Stolen treasure ...

Falco called for a rickshaw and headed in the other direction, to the Central Police Station on Foochow Road.

The headquarters of the Shanghai Municipal Police was busy, people shouting in several languages, both officers and visitors from a variety of ethnic backgrounds. Some Chinese carried what remained of their worldly possessions in bundles. Japanese officers were rude and arrogant, which was returned to them in kind in Chinese, with Sikh and British police trying to keep peace.

Falco asked to see William Ewart Fairbairn. The Sikh recognized him and motioned him to follow him down a hallway to an office.

The tall, gaunt man in his forties, with short gray hair, round spectacles, and a face showing the souvenirs of countless street fights, stood behind his desk and greeted Falco warmly with a smile and a fierce handshake.

"What trouble have you brought to Shanghai this time?"

"I'm looking for a killer with stolen temple artifacts," Falco said

A JOHNNY FALCO ADVENTURE

THE GOLD BUDDHA

WAYNE CAREY

WWW.BOLDVENTUREPRESS.COM

Audrey Parente, editor

Book design and cover by Rich Harvey

Bold Venture Press paperback edition, May 2026.

ISBN Paperback: 978-1-966085-47-8

ISBN eBook: 978-1-966085-48-5

Available in electronic edition.

To my grandson,

Akira Michael Carey-Allen

THE GOLD BUDDHA

Singapore

January 1932

1

In the China District of Singapore, John Falco entered the small, discrete tea shop, which was merely entitled Wong's Teas in English letters on the wooden plaque above the door. In the streets, the smell of fish permeated the air from the rivers and from the sampans delivering fish to the docks and taking them out to the waiting ships, and from the street vendors. But once inside Wong's shop, the sweet smell of teas and spices reigned.

Falco, dressed in a simple brown suit and a brown fedora, stood out among the locals because of his clothing and his facial features. He was white but usually was ignored because his size and build did not impose a threat, and his demeanor was always pleasant. Looks were often deceiving.

At the moment, only one other white was in the tea shop … an older man in a linen suit and a thin black tie, sitting at a back table, his straw Panama hat resting next to a steaming tea pot. As he sipped from a ceramic cup held in both bands, his pudgy face eased into a grateful smile and his blue eyes fluttered shut in appreciation. Strands of white hair stuck out from the sides of his otherwise bald head, flying errant from when he had removed his hat. He faced the door and the rest of the shop. A second, empty cup sat on the table opposite him.

Falco saw him immediately, the white suit like a beacon among Chinese and Malayan patrons.

He approached the table and gave a small bow.

"Colonel Butler."

Butler's right hand released the tea cup and he motioned to the seat with the empty tea cup.

"Falco, dear boy. Please sit down. Help yourself. Wong's tea is the best on the island. Mrs. Wong has been brewing it for decades. Sit down. How are your accommodations at the Raffles?"

"They're fine, sir."

"Gorgeous hotel, the Raffles. Too bad it's fallen on hard times during these economic troubles. Still, they try to keep up with their quality. Film stars and political figures still visit, but not as many as before."

Falco sat down and poured himself tea from the decorative pot. The lacquer cranes did not match the cherry blossoms on the cups. The oolong's aromatic steam filled his nostrils. He took a sip and nodded in appreciation.

"So, Colonel, you didn't ask me to Singapore just to sample the tea. What do you need?"

Butler set down his cup and smiled. "That's what I like about you, John. Always willing to help. Doesn't matter that I send for you to sail hundreds of miles from Hong Kong, no reason why. You just drop whatever you're doing and come."

"I booked a plane," Falco explained. "And I happen to be between … jobs." He took another sip.

"Here's the problem, my boy. There are a number of Buddhist temples in Singapore and surrounding areas within the Straits Settlement. It seems that some of their artifacts have been disappearing. In fact, a lot of artifacts. All precious metals. Gold, silver. Some with stones. Statues of Buddha. Gold cups. Some very old, some not so old. All very valuable. Maybe not so much individually, but collectively it adds up. And not a whisper of any being sold."

Falco set his cup down. "Curious. And you want me to use my contacts to see if any of these items have been sold on the black market, maybe to unscrupulous collectors."

"That's the general idea. I know back in the states your family is associated with those famous American gangster the cinema likes to romanticize in the motion pictures, but you …"

Falco frowned and his brown eyes held a glint of steel. His jaw tightened. "My father is one of those famous gangsters, what would be called a mob boss. He's in the newspapers all the time. My mother … passed away when I was sixteen and I left. She never wanted me involved in that business and I never was. She wanted the same for my older brother, but he seemed to have taken to it. I haven't associated with any of them since I left. And they have nothing to do with me. I seriously doubt that the New York mobsters are involved with stolen temple artifacts."

Butler chuckled. "No, of course not. But you do know people, don't you? On this side of the world."

"I have met my share," Falco admitted.

"Then you'll lend a hand? The governor has been anxious to solve this trouble, not that Buddhists tend to be militant but there could be some unrest in certain quarters. Makes the colony unstable."

Falco felt they were being watched. He eased into a different position in his chair and caught a glimpse of four Malayan laborers sitting at a nearby table, all ignoring their tea and watching the two white men seated at this back table as though they were intruders. While he listened to Butler, he concentrated on the Malayans, trying to catch a snippet of conversation, but they were not talking. Merely sitting, staring at them, and letting their tea get cold. Falco had not even noticed any steam rising from their cups, so they never poured any from the pot in the center of their table. If they did not come for Mrs. Wong's tea, why were they in the shop? Or had the presence of two white men so disturbed them that it put them off their drinks?

"Perhaps we should leave," Falco offered. "Come back to the Raffles with me and I'll buy you lunch."

Butler drained his cup. "An excellent idea. And on the way, we can stop at my office. I can give you a list we have of the stolen items. Probably not a complete list, as some of the locals don't always like talking to government officials."

As they stood, the four laborers pushed back their chairs in unison, making one loud scraping sound. They blocked the way to the exit.

Falco smiled at them and spoke in Chinese, since they were in the China District and his Malay was limited.

"Is there a problem?"

The first one pulled a knife, long and sharp. The others made menacing expressions.

Falco spun and kicked the Malayan's hand. The knife flew from numb fingers, the tip burrowing into the ceiling planks.

With another spin, Falco's foot caught the man in the side of the face, snapping his head around. The Malayan staggered into another table, knocking over tea cups and making two customers hurry away.

Around the room, other patrons began leaving discretely. The elderly Mrs. Wong came from the back room, wiping her hands on a towel, to see what caused the commotion.

The heel of Falco's right hand caught the second Malayan under the chin, sending him backward to the floor among a tangle of chairs.

The third came around the table, swinging at Falco, but he ducked and blocked the punches, and then fired a barrage of fists so fast that his strikes were blurs. The man staggered back against his table, his face bloody, his eyes already swelling. His falling body tipped the table, shatter the tea pot and the four empty cups, eliciting a scream from Mrs. Wong.

The last man hurled a knife through the air, but his aim was past Falco.

Turning, he saw the rusty blade bury itself in the chest of Eustace Butler. The Colonel's eyes widened in surprise and he slumped back into the chair he had just vacated. His arms fell limp at his sides and his head lulled back. A circle of red appeared around the blade, soaking his white shirt and linen jacket.

Falco ran to him, cradling the older man, calling his name. But Butler's eyes were already growing dull.

When Falco turned with a growl to the killers, all four men had vanished. Mrs. Wong was screaming in Chinese, and police whistles were blowing. The tea shop was empty except for Mrs. Wong, Falco, and Butler's slumped body.

2

"You killed Colonel Butler!" the police inspector accused.

Falco had been arrested by two Sikh police constables because there were only two people in the tea shop other than the body of the colonel. A hysterical Mrs. Wong told the officers that Falco fought with a number of her customers, broke tables, chairs, and pottery, and that knives were involved. She had pointed to the one still in the ceiling. Confused, the two officers cuffed Falco. Other officers were brought to the scene, and two Malay officers took him to the Beach Road police station, where he was processed and placed in a cell. At least the police station was new, constructed the previous year, so the accommodations were cleaner than Falco had encountered on other similar occasions. He sat on the cot, his back to the cool brick wall with legs crossed and eyes closed in contemplation. When Malayan officers took him to an interrogation room to be questioned by a British police inspector, his mind had organized his own questions with what little Butler had told him.

"Of course I didn't," Falco answered calmly. "He was killed by four Malayan assassins who either followed him or knew he would be at Wong's Tea Shop. Unless he was working on a case more prominent than the stolen temple artifacts, he was targeted because of the thefts. He was going to show me his paperwork on the case."

The inspector, a large man in his early forties with a long, lined face browned from the sun, gray peppering his black hair, and brown eyes creased from constant squinting, scoffed at Falco.

"You aren't any kind of colonial official. According to your passport, you are an American living in Hong Kong. You don't even have an occupation. As far as I know, you are the thief and I'll see you hang for murdering Colonel Butler. And don't deny it. We have witnesses."

"Witness," Falco corrected. "You have one witness, a distraught woman who speaks very little English."

"You seem to know a lot for someone who just arrived in Singapore."

The inspector opened Falco's passport, then tossed it on the desk between them.

"Why did you come here from Hong Kong? What kind of business are you in?"

"Eustace Butler was a friend of mine. He wired me to come to Singapore to help him in the matter of the stolen artifacts."

The inspector placed his hand on the passport, his fingers flipping through the pages. He shook his head. "I very much doubt that. What you mentioned is a matter for the colonial police, not some young American vagrant. According to your papers you are twenty-five and you've done extensive traveling. Back and forth between Hong Kong and America, Hawaii, Japan, Shanghai. A number of times to Singapore. Just what is your business, Mr. Falco?"

"I am a consultant."

"For what?"

Falco shrugged, rattling the handcuffs that bound his wrists. "For many things. Thefts, kidnappings, murders."

The policeman scowled. "Sounds like you're the thief and the kidnapper and the murderer."

Falco sat back, resting his cuffed hands on his lap. His right hand covered the cuff on his left wrist and toyed with the restraint. "And it sounds like you have a very narrow perspective, Inspector. You must not be very successful in your career. You have a number of convictions that have not been held up, am I right? Disciplinary actions, correct? You're pushing very hard, but in the wrong direction. Why don't you give Inspector-General Harold Fairburn a call and mention me?"

The inspector's brown face flushed bright red. His right hand curled into a fist which he shook at Falco. "Just settle down, boy! No one is bothering the Inspector-General over the likes of you. You're mine and

I'll see you convicted and hung for murder!"

He called for the Sikh constable who had been standing guard just outside the interrogation room. "Take this man back to his cell."

Falco stood up slowly. "Then I won't be needing these."

He dropped the unlocked handcuffs onto the table, next to his passport. The inspector looked from the cuffs to Falco, his jaw slack.

3

When the Sikh constable came for Falco two days later, he opened the cell door and motioned him forward.

"No handcuffs?" Falco asked.

The Sikh humphed, his mouth a straight line under his thick beard, then motioned with a tip of his turbaned head for Falco to proceed him.

This time, he was not taken to an interrogation room but to an office.

The police inspector stood to one side of the desk, though from the photographs on the desk and wall, it was clearly his office. Seated behind the desk was a middle-aged man of military bearing, his graying hair cut short, his clean-shaven face creased with lines of strength and determination. He was a tall, slender man with a fit, commanding figure.

"Good morning, Inspector-General," Falco said with a bow of his head.

Harold Fairburn stood up and reached a hand over the desk to grip Falco's in a hearty, welcoming shake.

"Falco! Good to see you, old boy. Sorry for this little mix-up."

As he sat back in the leather chair, he gave a disapproving glare to the police inspector.

Without being offered, Falco took one of the two chairs on his side of the desk and smiled.

"No harm done, sir."

The police inspector refused to meet Falco's eyes. His jaw squeezed tight, his own eyes cold, looking everywhere in the small room except at the other two occupants. The Sikh eased the door shut and left.

"Any word on Colonel Butler's killers?" Falco asked.

"I'm afraid not, Falco," Fairburn said, elbows on the desk, hands folded in front of him. "This investigation was not handled properly. The four men in your statement could be anywhere by now. Sumatra, Java, anywhere. I doubt they stayed on the island. We might have rounded up one or two of them if this had been done competently."

The standing inspector closed his eyes briefly, his face flushing.

"You knew Colonel Butler consulted me?" Falco asked.

Fairburn shook his head. "No, that was all on his own, though I heartily approve. He was working under orders directly from Sir Cecil Clementi. The governor filled me in on the case, mentioned that Butler was bringing in an outsider. He didn't mention you by name. Sir Cecil is not pleased you were arrested in this debacle."

"Simple miscommunication," Falco offered.

"Well, it's set us back. In the meantime, other artifacts have been stolen. The Buddhist community is causing a stir."

"If I could see Colonel Butler's file. He was going to show it to me before he was killed."

Fairburn waved his right hand dismissively. "No need. I have it here. Had it delivered before I came. Thought it might be useful." His long fingers tapped a folder in the center of the desk.

"May I?" Falco asked.

Fairburn slid the folder toward him.

Falco opened the folder and glanced through the collection of papers. Several police reports, lists of stolen articles from separate Buddhist temples throughout Singapore and the Straits Settlement. Names of priests and monks. As Falco perused the lists of stolen items, he wondered when this was noticed. An occasional gold Buddha figure now and then, from numerous temples. Ceremonial pieces that just weren't there when they were needed. Considering the months from the time the first thefts were noticed, Falco understood why the police had not taken the situation seriously. Small items at first, then the thefts became more brazen.

"The last page is an addendum I had put in," Fairburn added. "Something that came through within the past day."

Falco took the sheet out and read it. A note filed from the Lian Shan Shuang Lin Monastery. This time the missing artifact was not some small statue or article that might go unnoticed. It was a life-size Buddha covered in gold, less than three feet tall, seated in a lotus position, referred to as the Venerable Monk Shi.

"I'd like to pay a visit to the monastery," Falco said as he tucked the papers back in place and closed the folder.

"Attend to that later. I'll have someone drive you. But first, you need to return to your hotel room for a bath, a shave, and some fresh clothes. Butler's funeral is this afternoon. Sir Cecil himself will be attending."

The white tower of Saint Andrew's Cathedral stood high in the bright blue sky, overlooking the church yard. Two dozen people circled around one open grave, where an oak casket lay suspended, a British flag draped over it. An Anglican priest stood at the head of the grave and made his remarks about the departed.

Falco stood at the back, hat in hand. He saw Harold Fairburn with Sir Cecil Clementi, Governor of the Straits Settlements. Falco had never met Sir Cecil but knew of him when he was governor of Hong Kong until two years ago. He was a tall, straight man with a long face and a strong jaw. He stood with hands clasped in front of him, head bowed.

Falco glanced at other mourners. Most were Europeans in suits. The few women present wore black dresses, two with veils. They appeared to be the wives of men within the ranks of government officials. On the periphery was a lone nun. At first Falco didn't realize that she was among the mourners until he noticed that her white habit was from a Catholic order, not Anglican.

When the priest concluded his prayer, the crowd began to disperse.

Fairburn came toward Falco, Clementi at his side.

"Falco, I was speaking to Sir Cecil about your connection with this affair. Sir Cecil, this is John Falco."

The tall governor reached out his hand. Falco could tell he wasn't impressed. To the statesman, Falco was far too young to have any experience and knowledge, a small, slender man that didn't seem to have any importance. Falco took his hand and put pressure in the grip. Not enough to break fingers but enough to demonstrate that he had more strength in his frame than the governor gave him credit. Sir Cecil's white eyebrows rose with a glimmer of respect.

"So you're the young fellow who intends to settle this matter," Clementi said in a tone that suggested his was false boasting on Falco's part. "Eustace Butler served His Majesty for decades and was a skilled investigator. Yet he comes to you for help and gets himself killed."

"I regret that, Sir Cecil," Falco said.

"Falco has helped in a number of cases over the past couple of years," Fairburn put in. "Surely you recall some reports that would have come your way when you were in Hong Kong. Just last year he located the kidnapped daughter of a United States senator and he helped the Hong Kong police solve a murder, which somehow involved the Nanking government."

Clementi raised one eyebrow. "That was you? My impression was of an older man. I was told that it was someone who had studied with Shaolin monks."

Falco gave a modest bow of his head. "I was allowed to live and train at the temple when I was sixteen, Sir Cecil. I spent only five years among the monks."

Clementi lifted his head and studied Falco with a glint in his eye. "An American Shaolin. Now that is something of a curiosity. So, you think you can solve this matter and find Butler's killers?"

Falco took a deep breath. "The killers have already been found, Sir Cecil, which is why I was a bit late for the services. My apologies. I'm afraid I missed the service inside the cathedral and only made it to the graveside."

"What's this?" Fairburn asked, surprised.

"Yes, sir. The constable you assigned to me, Sukha Singh, informed me that four bodies were fished out of the Kallang River this morning. Sukha Singh knew that four men attacked Colonel Butler and myself and mentioned the discovery to me when he came to pick me up at the Raffles. I insisted we take a look at these bodies, which had been taken to the Changi Hospital morgue. These were four Malayans and did not warrant much police attention because of their deaths. When I examined the bodies I recognized the four men from the tea shop. I left a few mementos of our meeting on their persons, bruises and abrasions from our encounter. Certainly not enough to cause death some days later."

Clementi nodded slowly. "How did these four die, then?"

"Poison."

"Poison!" echoes Fairburn. "Are you sure?"

Falco shrugged. "Without doing a proper analysis, yes. No trauma to the bodies, but pink lividity and a bitter almond smell, despite being in the river since last night. All four men must have been poisoned at the same time, probably given in drinks, and their bodies dumped in the river. The bodies weren't weighted down, so they stayed together in the current."

"Curious," Clementi mused. "You seem to know your stuff, young man."

Fairburn smiled. "He's full of surprises, isn't he? I have the utmost confidence in young Falco."

"Good work, Falco," the governor said. "Now we can put the tragic murder to rest. Obviously these hoodlums fell to misadventure because of their criminal lifestyle. Hopefully you can handle the matter of the stolen items just as quickly. I'll allow you to keep on with the case, if you are willing, since Butler had confidence in you."

"Ah, Sir Cecil, if I may? Colonel Butler was not killed out of chance. These four men went to that tea shop specifically to murder him, and perhaps me in the bargain. They had no intention of robbing him but to kill him. And then their deaths were done to foil further investigation into who had hired them. They might have been used in the thefts or they might have only been hired for the colonel's murder. I don't know yet. But finding the killers is only the beginning. There is a complex plot that needs to be exposed."

Clementi pursed his lips and turned toward the inspector-general. "Fairburn, you are in charge of this matter. See that this young man has whatever he needs to solve this case. I don't care if you personally become his driver. Whatever he needs."

He reached out his hand toward Falco.

"Mr. Falco, under the circumstances it has been a pleasure meeting you. You have the resources of the Straits Settlement at your disposal. I trust you will not disappoint us."

Falco watched the other mourners disperse, the cars start to pull away from the curbside. Clementi parted company with Fairburn and climbed into the back seat of a black sedan with an aide while the driver started the machine and pulled into the street. Fairburn drove his own automobile.

The last of the gathering was the Catholic nun who had hung back from the others. She approached Falco as he watched the governor and the inspector-general leave in their respective cars. He heard the swish of her starched white habit as she walked over the old stone path.

"Was that Governor Clementi?" she asked.

He turned slowly toward her. She appeared in her thirties, her blue eyes squinting at the bright sun. A layer of perspiration glistened her forehead. She was an attractive woman with a pleasant, narrow face, pale despite the tropics, thin even under the habit. Falco guessed she spent most of her days in prayer rather than enjoying the weather. She stretched a long, thin hand toward him.

"Sister Catherine."

He took the hand. "John Falco. And yes, that was the governor. Did you know Colonel Butler?"

She nodded as she lower her head. "Such a tragedy."

"He wasn't Catholic," Falco stated with blatant curiosity.

She gave a small smile. "Obviously. We crossed paths several times in my work with the local people."

Falco motioned to the Sikh constable standing rigidly near the last black sedan waiting at the side of the road, the car that had been granted to him by the inspector-general. "If you don't mind, I have some business. It was nice meeting you, Sister."

4

The Lian Shan Shuang Lin Monastery, located in the Toa Payoh district of central Singapore, was the Twin Grove of the Lotus Mountain Temple, which referred to the sala trees in India where Buddha attained enlightenment. Built in 1907 by the wealthy merchant Low Kim Pong, its flaring red terracotta roofs and white pillars reminded Falco of the Shaolin monastery where he had lived and trained for five years, where he had left his troubled, angry youth to travel on a different path. Visiting the temple brought him a nostalgic sense of peace.

He left Sukha Singh waiting at the car and passed through the nine feet tall main gate, the Mountain Gate, and headed toward the main entrance, the Hall of Celestial Kings. An elderly monk stood in front of the doors carved with flowers, birds, and symbols of longevity. He smiled calmly and bowed his shaven head to Falco.

"May I help you, honored guest?" he asked in English.

"Venerable father," Falco replied in Chinese, "I am John Falco. I am investigating the thefts of the temple materials."

The monk tilted his head slightly but did not react to Falco's use of Chinese. His smile faded and his eyes took on a sadness.

"My son, I am Wai Yim, abbot to this humble monastery. I will help in any way I can in the return of Brother Shi to the Temple."

"That is the gold Buddha statue that was recently stolen?" Falco asked.

"Yes. Brother Shi lived a hundred years ago. He was a spiritual leader here in Singapore and helped the poor. He had been a wealthy Chinese who forsook his wealth to feed the starving. He went into the hills to achieve enlightenment, and then served the people until he was very old. Now he dwells within the statue. He has spent his years watching over villages from different small shrines and temples. When the Twin Grove of the Lotus Mountain Temple was built, he was brought here, though he was to return on his journey to visit all the smaller temples to give his blessings. Come, I will show you where he has rested before he was taken."

They entered the hall through the carved doors, past the statues of the three seated Buddhas, and into the gardens beyond. Wai Yim nodded to other monks as they entered the next hall, the Mahavira Hall, and passed through toward the last of the halls, the Sutra Hall.

The abbot bowed to the thirty foot high copper statue of the goddess Guan Yin, with her many hands fanning out and her thousand eyes looking on, the personification of compassion. Falco contemplated that if all those eyes, and those of the hundreds of copper statues of Buddha around them, could have seen the theft, the goddess could speak who would commit such a crime. But she sat in silence.

To the right was a stone pedestal about three feet high, flanked by small statues and urns of brass. The stone stand was conspicuous because it was empty. Wai Yim motioned to it.

"Here is where our Honored Brother Shi rested on his journey."

"And this statue was covered with gold?" Falco asked.

"He was within the gold Buddha, yes."

Which would have been heavy, Falco reasoned, not something someone could tuck under his arm and walk away with. More likely several men, perhaps four, like the rough looking characters who ended up poisoned and floating in the Kallang River. A small group of laborers would go unnoticed, though not to the monks,unless their theft had been in the middle of the night. Doors were not locked and the halls were not guarded.

"Was anything else missing?" Falco asked.

The abbot shrugged. "Nothing was noticed. Our hearts are broken that our Brother Shi has been taken."

"But other items have gone missing before."

"Yes. Small statues. Always those covered in gold leaf or made of gold or silver."

"Do you suspect anyone within the monastery?"

Wai Yim shook his head. "I know every monk and I know every person who works here. I cannot say anything about visitors. Our temple is large and many people come from all over the world. We have many visitors each day. Americans like yourself. British. Europeans. Japanese. And many Chinese and Malays."

Falco stepped to the open doors and looked at the buildings to the right and left of the hall. "Those are residential buildings, aren't they?"

"Yes. To the left is where I live."

"And did you or any other monk hear anything during the night?"

"Nothing that disturbed our sleep."

These thieves moved like the legendary ninja of Japan, but Falco doubted anyone of the Buddhist faith would have defiled a temple.

Falco noticed a white figure moving across the garden from the Mahavira Hall toward the Sutra Hall. A Catholic nun was so out of place in this setting, surrounded by statues of Buddhas and goddesses and stone lion-dog guardians that Falco thought at first it must be an illusion, a trick of the sun sinking toward the West. Then he recognized the pale narrow face and blue eyes of Sister Catherine.

"So nice to see you again, Mr. Falco."

The Sister bowed a greeting to the abbot.

"I am sorry for disturbing you, Wai Yim."

The monk inclined his head, smiled and spoke in thickly accented English. "It is always a pleasure when you visit, Sister Catherine. Do you know Mr. Falco?"

"We met under more austere circumstances, Abbot. May I ask, Mr. Falco, if your visit to the temple is connected with Colonel Butler's murder?"

Falco wondered what Sister Catherine's interest should be. "In a way, but I can't really discuss it."

The nun gave a dismissive wave of her hand. "The theft of the gold Buddha? Such a tragedy. And all those other thefts. Small and insignificant compared with the gold Buddha. Colonel Butler was investigating the thefts. Does that mean you have taken over the investigation? You were talking with the governor at the funeral."

"And you are rather curious for a nun," Falco pointed out.

She flashed a smile and shrugged. "It's a failing of mine. I have prayed about it, but apparently God wants me to use it. I keep saying to myself, Kate, you shouldn't be poking your nose in where it doesn't belong, but there I go again. There was a village in India that was only a rumor, and I couldn't let it go until I found out where it was, and it was a good thing, too, because the well had gone bad and the whole village was sick and needed medical attention. If I hadn't been so curious everyone would have died. *He* had a plan and it included my curiosity." She pointed a finger skyward.

Wai Yim motioned toward her but spoke to Falco in Chinese. "Sister Catherine has been helping at the temples throughout Singapore, especially with children. She has found medical help for many."

"Do you have medical training, Sister?" Falco asked. "The abbot told me you help the locals."

"Yes, I know. Oh, I speak a little Chinese, I'm just not very good at it. I also speak a little Malayan and even Hindi. That's the trouble with our order. I can be sent anywhere in the world. But I have a good ear for languages, just not a good mouth. I don't always get the pronunciations down. Anyway, to answer your question, yes I do have medical training. I had just finished nursing school when I took my vows. Sometimes I'm attached to a doctor, more often I am by myself to evaluate the medical needs of an area. I've been all over the Straits Settlement. Which is how I know about the thefts of temple articles. And I noticed this one person happens to be in the area around the time of the thefts. One man who shows up for no reason. Then he's gone and so are some gold statues."

Falco perked up. He was beginning to wonder how he might slip away from the Sister without upsetting her feelings, but now he became interested. Perhaps her incessant talking and her overactive curiosity might be useful.

"What man? Do you have a name?"

"Serge something. He's a Russian. Rough looking character. Very unkempt. Always wears a wrinkled white linen suit and a straw Panama hat. Shaggy black hair and he always needs a shave. Smokes those dreadful skinny cigars. He sells things to the local villages, usually liquor. Filthy stuff."

Falco took a calming breath. "You didn't happen to hear his last name?"

"Yes. It's either Smirnoff or Ivanoff or Romanoff or something like that. Or was it Kuzoff? I'm sorry, I didn't catch it. I wasn't close enough. But the first name is definitely Serge."

Falco shook his head. "That isn't much to go on."

She straightened stiffly and raised indignant eyebrows. "Well, why don't you ask him yourself? He's booked passage on a steamship that leaves tomorrow. I saw him again on the streets and followed him. I saw him go into the office of the Straits Steamship Company. I could see him through the window. When he left, I approached the clerk. He was British. So I asked if that was one of our parishioners, Serge, that I didn't know he was leaving so soon, and the clerk said tomorrow on the *Queen of Sumatra*. He wasn't very cooperative after that and I couldn't very well ask what the man's last name was if I knew him as a parishioner, now could I?"

"Thank you, Sister," Falco said, processing the information. "You've been very helpful."

She grinned at him. "Are you going to arrest him?"

"There's hardly any evidence to do that. No, I'll continue the investigation."

"Will you book passage and trail him? Is he a suspect?"

"A person of interest, shall we say."

She clapped her hands together. "Marvelous. You see, the Lord works in mysterious ways. He used my sense of curiosity to follow that man, and I found a clue for you. I was helpful, wasn't I?"

"Indispensable. Now, good evening, Sister. I've a lot to do. And thank you."

Sukha Singh accompanied Falco into the Straits Steamship Company offices in the curved, five story tall Ocean Building on Collyer Quay. The hour was late and most of the company headquarter offices were closed, but the clerks dealing with customers were still available for passage. Seeing the Sikh police officer lent some air of officiousness to Falco's presence. Because of his age and less imposing demeanor, he was not always taken seriously. With the tall, dour policeman standing behind him, just to the left, he was able to grab the first clerk's attention.

"I'm working with the Singapore police. There is a person of interest who has booked passage for tomorrow on the *Queen of Sumatra*."

The clerk was a man in his thirties with a thick, drooping mustache. "I'm sorry, but we can't give out information concerning passengers."

Falco could not see Sukha Singh, but he sensed movement from the man. A slight intake of air, the quiet rustle of his uniform as he straightened. He could not see the constable's bearded face, but something in it made the eyes of the clerk shoot toward him. The clerk's face whitened and his eyes widened, mouth hanging open. He began to stutter when his attention returned to Falco.

"Under normal conditions, that is … sir. What, um, is the name of the party?" He pulled a book from under the counter and flipped it open.

"I'm afraid I don't know the full name. I was hoping you could help. He is a Russian whose first name is Serge. Tall, long hair. He came in this afternoon."

The clerk nodded enthusiastically. "I remember. Here he is. Serge Petrov, Russian citizen. A merchant, he claimed. He is shipping some delicate cargo with him. He is traveling to Shanghai, sailing tomorrow afternoon. He booked passage for himself and three others."

"Are there any staterooms available?"

"Yes sir. One."

"Book me passage, please."

Falco arrived early to the *Queen of Sumatra*. He found his cabin, dropped off his small bag with his change of clothes, and strolled the decks. He located the stateroom assigned to Serge Petrov on the upper deck, listened carefully from the passageway, but could not determine if anyone was inside. Then he went out to watch the various activities on the ship. Passengers arrived, crew busied themselves with various tasks. While leaning on the rail of the upper deck, he saw a truck arrive. Behind it pulled a taxi, out of which climbed a tall, slender man in a wrinkled white linen suit.

Falco studied Serge Petrov. He had the bearing of a soldier, a no-nonsense arrogant attitude, yet he was unkempt. Shaggy hair, unshaven face. His Panama hat shaded his eyes but Falco felt the predatory look as he gazed over the dock and the waiting ship.

The second passenger slid from the back seat of the cab. This was a Chinese woman wearing a gold *qipao* style dress slit to her knees, her black hair short and curled into waves. She appeared to be only about thirty but she carried herself as though she were older and more important than anyone else. She stood beside the Russian with an imperious air. She was no servant or even a subservient wife. She was an equal, a partner perhaps, or even one who was in charge.

From the other side of the taxi's rear seat and from the front passenger side came two bookends. Squat, square looking men in tan suits. Rough faces and thick arms, large hands calloused from years of manual labor. Their jackets were ill-fitting enough to show the outline of revolvers tucked into holsters at their hips.

The passenger of the truck climbed down and circled to the back of the vehicle. He was a Chinese in laborer clothes and worn sandals. He threw aside the tarp over the back of the truck, revealing several wooden crates and two other Chinese waiting on top of them. One jumped down and the second began easing the first crate out to be grabbed by his companions.

Petrov hovered over the three laborers, giving unnecessary directions. The three appeared to know what they were doing, that they had done so hundreds of times, and aside from one giving a slight roll of his eyes, they remained stoic and expressionless.

Falco leaned on the upper rail of the ship, watching the men move the first crate toward the ramp of the ship, his eyes shaded by his brown fedora. He noticed other passengers moving about. One was a woman, at least ten years his senior, in her mid thirties. She was dressed in a conservative long khaki skirt coming to the tops of her ankle boots, and a khaki jacket belted at her slim waist. A sun hat sat on her wavy blonde hair. She approached him from the right and settled next to him to lean on the rail.

"That's him," she said. "That's Serge."

Falco's head snapped to the right.

"Sister Catherine?"

He hadn't recognized the nun out of her habit.

"Oh, don't look so shocked. We are women under those habits and we don't have to wear them all the time. I've already informed my order that I would be taking a sabbatical. I explained that I would be assisting the colonial government on a special matter. Mother Superior is very understanding. I cannot very well show up in my habit. Mister Serge would recognize me. After all, I've seen him at two of the villages and then at the shipping office. If he sees me as I now am, he probably won't recognize me."

"Sister Catherine," Falco began, frowning at her, "you cannot come along. This could be very dangerous."

She gave a soft chuckle. "I've been in dangerous situations a number of times. Headhunters, pirates. I've been in the middle of revolutions. This is merely a sea voyage to China. Oh, look. They're taking the first crate to the cargo hold."

Falco turned back to see that a crane was lifting the wooden container off the deck, lowering it through a hatchway to the dark bowels of the ship.

"Do you think the gold Buddha is in one of those crates, Mr. Falco?"

"Sister Catherine, I —"

"Call me Kate, please. After all, I am not wearing my habit. I'm an ordinary person right now."

"Okay. Kate. I don't know if any of those crates have any contraband in them. Not until they are opened and I don't have any authority to open them and the authorities don't have any evidence to warrant opening them." He had spoken to Fairburn, and he was willing to examine the crates before they were placed on the ship until he discovered that they belonged to a Russian citizen. By the time the proper papers were filed, the ship would have sailed. He had approved of Falco's plan to follow Petrov to Shanghai.

"Then we'll just have to sneak into the hold and open one."

Falco took a deep breath. Despite that actually being his intention, he was not about to let anyone know it. "Kate, you cannot get involved. Please allow me to investigate."

"But haven't I helped you?"

"Yes."

"Hasn't my information been invaluable?"

"Yes."

"Then I may still be of use. I'm not going to ignore everything during the voyage."

"You aren't going to be on this voyage. You're getting off before we sail."

She gave him a hurt expression. "But I already have passage. I'm not going to throw that away. It would be wasteful and look suspicious."

She looked at her wristwatch, then patted his arm. "I tell you what. You keep an eye on Serge and his group while I wander around the ship. Is that woman with him? Maybe I can find out who she is, unless you already know. I didn't think so. I haven't seen her before. We sail in about an hour and I want to find the dining room and see what's for lunch. I'll see you later in your stateroom."

She was off before he could protest. He could cause a scene, but that would get him noticed. He could go to the captain, have her removed from the ship, but he was a civilian consultant of the colonial government. He had no authority. More than likely, the crew would toss him off for making a fuss. As long as she didn't make herself conspicuous or expose him in any way, perhaps he could keep his distance from her, avoid her. After all, it would not be a long voyage to Shanghai.

5

Falco watched while all three crates were loaded on board ship and stored in the aft cargo hold. The three Chinese laborers piled into the truck and drove off. Serge Petrov led his group up the gangway to find their cabins. The two armed men followed, glaring at other passengers and crew. The woman walked a pace behind Petrov with the attitude they were escorting her. Falco was curious as to her role in this affair. The most important objective was to determine if the stolen temple artifacts, particularly the life-size gold Buddha, were hidden in those crates. That would prove that Petrov was behind the thefts. Then he could notify the Straits Settlement authorities, who would arrange for someone to meet the *Queen of Sumatra* at either Hong Kong or Shanghai and take Petrov into custody. If all went well, Petrov and his mysterious lady friend would never meet Falco and he would have no need to confront any of them.

The crew cast off lines, and the ship began its slow move to open water.

As the ship sailed away from Singapore, Falco strolled back to his cabin. A few hours of exercising and a quiet meal in his room, and then he would pay a visit to the cargo hold in the middle of the night.

Unlocking the door, he stepped into the stateroom. It was a mid-sized cabin, with a table, chairs and two bunks built into the bulkheads on either side. A washroom opened to the left and a porthole let in light. It wasn't elegant but neither was it cramped and austere.

He did not expect to see Sister Catherine seated at the table, book in hand, reading, her sun hat resting on the table.

"Sister Catherine!"

"Kate," she corrected, closing her book and laying it aside.

"What are you doing here?"

"As I told you, I am here to assist you."

"I mean in my cabin."

"Oh, that. I'm afraid I may have misled the steward. When I booked passage, they said there were no more cabins available. I told them that I would be sharing your accommodations. I explained that I was your sister. I'm certain they took that in a totally different context, but since there are two bunks in this cabin, arrangements were made."

"This isn't appropriate."

"But I assure you, it is. A few days of sharing a cabin would not ruin either of our reputations. No one would consider anything but a platonic relationship between us, taking in our age differences. What anyone sees is an older sister and a younger brother. Besides, I know you are a complete gentleman."

"You don't know me at all, Sister," Falco pointed out.

She smiled and wiggled a finger at him. "But I know your spirit. And I spoke to Abbot Wai Yim about you. He has heard of you. You're a Shaolin, aren't you?"

Falco frowned at her. "There has to be other accommodations. Perhaps there is another woman passenger who would consider a companion."

She shook her head.

"Then I will find something else."

He made a move toward his leather bag sitting near the cabin door.

"Wouldn't that get you noticed by the people you are investigating?" she asked.

He thought for a moment. This was very inconvenient. Sister Catherine had inserted herself into his investigation. She meant well but her interference could disrupt everything. He couldn't get rid of her, couldn't alter the situation. He pushed back his annoyance. Anger would solve nothing. Perhaps he could even use her in some way. He could stay in the cabin, away from view, and she could ask discrete questions or surreptitiously keep an eye on Petrov and his entourage.

He calmed his spirit before he spoke. "Very well. Until something else can be arranged, you may stay. But speak to no one, especially Serge Petrov and the people with him. Do not let anyone know that I am here to investigate him and his cargo. Not a word, not a hint."

"Of course, Mr. Falco. Oh, perhaps I should start calling you John if people are to believe I am your sister."

"Just don't talk to anyone. That's the best scenario."

"But hardly practical. You might be able to stay in this cabin the whole voyage but I must get out, have fresh air, and see people. Don't worry. I won't tell anyone you are a detective. The same as I won't tell anyone I am a nun. That makes people uncomfortable. They are less likely to open up. You should see how people change their attitudes when I show up in my habit. Don't worry. I won't compromise you. I'm here to help."

She grinned at him. He did not feel reassured.

Sister Catherine went to the dining room and joined the other passengers for dinner as evening fell, while Falco had a steward bring him a plate of vegetables and some bread. Then he slipped out of the cabin and prowled the passageways of the ship. He heard the activity in the dining room, the chatter of people and the clinking of utensils and plates. Several passengers were also enjoying the amenities of the nearby bar.

Falco climbed down into the bowels of the ship and found the cargo hold. Crew members passed him, but no one gave him any more attention than a nod.

He took a small flash light from his jacket pocket when he entered the cavernous cargo hold. Dozens of crates and trunks piled on each other were lashed down and secured in place. The narrow beam of his light played across the cargo. He found merchandise from Singapore being sent to Shanghai, machinery, engine parts for aircraft, weapons, cloth, seeds. Some trunks were stored for passengers, the luggage not needed during the voyage. There were crates of books for schools, bibles for churches or missionaries. Then his beam flashed across three containers he recognized. Two of them three foot by two, the third a little larger, stacked on top of each other and covered with a cargo net that kept them snug against the aft bulkhead. He stared at them for a time, wondering how he might look inside of each. The black painted letters stenciled on the wood declared that their contents were fragile, glass.

Turning off his flashlight, he plunged the hold into blackness. He felt the roll of the deck on the gentle ocean waves, the rhythm of the water, heard the creak of the ship, the hum of the engines. Feeling his way, remembering how the stack of crates looked, he climbed the netting to the top container. His arm reached through the net and his fingers touched the top of the uppermost crate. His fingertips ran along the wood, felt the edges and the imperceptible space between the slats. At the corner, he pushed. The wood remained immobile. He concentrated and tensed the muscles of his fingers. The wood creaked. Nails groaned.

Falco pried the lid up and slipped his hand inside. He felt a mass of packing hay, then wormed his fingers through it to some solid object underneath. It was cold and smooth. His fingertips explored the surface, from the thin end, over its curve, to the wide middle. Then paper glued in place. A label. It was a bottle containing liquor. A quick exploration found two other bottles within reach, nestled in the protective straw.

Disappointed, he pulled out his arm and pushed the lid back in place.

Climbing down, he leaned his back against the crates and contemplated how he might examine the contents more thoroughly, especially the larger crate on the bottom.

He would need more time to remove the cargo netting, pry open the lid of the uppermost crate, and dig through its contents. If he found nothing but liquor bottles, he would need to search the other crates, requiring more time. He could not be disturbed by crew or passengers. A visit to the hold in the wee hours of morning, before sunrise, would eliminate passengers wandering down below, but there still would be crew making rounds. He hated to admit it, but he would have to enlist the aid of Sister Catherine.

She was an amiable woman, likable in a way and eager to help. He did not like her intrusion into his life, but he was willing to compromise since she had been helpful previously. At least she was no longer dressed in her habit. Even though she had worn one of all white for the tropical heat, he was still reminded of the nuns of his youth in New York. They had not been so amiable. His father was a powerful gangster even then, and the nuns and priests had always been eager to please him. Charles

Falco was generous to the church, as though he needed to buy his way into Heaven or to compensate for his many sins. The clergy overlooked his transgressions, as long as he confessed weekly. But to the younger son, they did not need to be nice. They did not have to pretend.

During his time at the Shaolin temple, throughout his training, he had been beaten with bamboo sticks, yelled at, forced to endure pain, but never out of hatred or anger. The monks had never shown anger. He could not say that about the nuns in the parochial schools.

Yet, Sister Catherine had not been like that. She had always been friendly, if a bit quirky. If he was to endure her presence, at least he could make use of her.

He reached the upper deck and passed along the ship's starboard railing with the goal of returning to his cabin. Other passengers strolled the gangways or lingered against the railing, watching the stars and crescent moon reflecting on the black waters. The dining hall was mostly empty, stewards removing plates and glassware from vacant tables. The chatter came from the bar, echoing in the night. Someone was singing an Irish song that made Falco think of his friend, Travis Flanagan, who should still be in Hong Kong and hopefully staying out of trouble.

He did not see the woman exiting the bar until he nearly collided with her.

"Mister Falco!" exclaimed a startled Sister Catherine. "I thought you were staying in the cabin. Good! You can join us."

"Kate, what are you doing?"

"Oh, just enjoying the company of some fellow passengers. Don't worry, I only had a little wine. Just one glass." But she held up two fingers.

She grabbed him by the wrist and pulled.

His instinct was to twist, push against her thumb to release her grip, but he had no desire to either hurt her or offend her. He reluctantly allowed himself to be guided through the doors of the bar as she wound her way among the crowd of patrons standing, talking, and drinking.

"I was having a lovely conversation with two of the passengers," she continued, "and had told them about you. I explained I was traveling with my brother. That's you. They were anxious to meet you. Especially the young lady."

She stopped suddenly at a table. Two people sat with glasses in their hands. Two other places at the table were empty, though a glass perched on the table at one vacated spot, a single drop of red wine stirred in the bottom of the glass by the gentle roll of the deck.

"Here he is!" she declared to the couple. "This is my brother, John Falco."

The sour expression on Serge Petrov brightened into a toothy smile and his long, lanky frame stood up as he reached out his hand.

The woman seated beside him looked up from her small glass of sherry to eye him and raise her eyebrows slightly in acknowledgment, her cold features losing a few degrees of their frigidness.

"A pleasure to meet you," Petrov said as they shook hands, his grip firm but not overpowering. "Your sister, Kate, has told us much about you."

The Russian waved his hand at one of the empty chairs. "Please, join us. Will you have a drink?"

Falco shot Sister Catherine a look but returned Petrov's smile. To refuse would draw suspicion. Besides, if he could draw the Russian into an innocent conversation he might be able to learn some pertinent information.

"Some tea would be nice, thank you," he said as he pulled the one chair out for Sister Catherine and took the next one, across from the Chinese woman whose smoldering eyes watched his every move.

"No wine or brandy?" Petrov asked. "How about some vodka?"

Falco shook his head. "Thank you, but I don't drink alcohol."

As Petrov sat, he motioned to his companion. "And may I introduce to you Mrs. Mie Lee."

"*Wo hen gaoxing renshi ni,*" Falco said in Chinese.

A smile threatened to curl the corners of her mouth. "You speak Mandarin very well, Mr. Falco," She said in perfect English. She slowly set her glass down. "I understand that you consider yourself some sort of expert on China."

"Expert, no. I have learned much the few years I have lived there, but I know I have much more to learn and I will never know enough to ever be considered an expert. Where are you from Mrs. Lee?" The tradition in China was to place the family name before the given name, but Falco believed Petrov was following European convention when he introduced the woman.

"Nanking. Have you been there?" she asked.

"Recently, yes."

"On business or pleasure?"

"Business," he replied, not elaborating. It would not go well if he explained his involvement in an incident involving the former president, Chiang Kai-shek.

"And what business are you in?" Petrov asked as he waved over a Malayan waiter.

"A little bit of everything," Falco answered.

As the Russian ordered another vodka and sherry for he and Mrs. Lee, he also asked for wine for Sister Catherine and a tea for Falco.

Petrov grinned at Falco after the waiter left. "Ah, me too. At the moment, I am salesman. Vodka, brandy, even wine. But with you, I would go broke."

Falco smiled at the Russian's joke.

"Your sister said her name was Murdoch," Mrs. Lee said. "Yet you are Falco."

Sister Katherine chimed in quickly. "My husband's name. My *late* husband. John insisted I come to the East to help me over the loss." She patted Falco's forearm resting on the table and smiled sadly at him.

Mie Lee nodded. "My condolences. I too am a widow, although my husband passed two years ago. He was a businessman in Nanking."

Falco wondered what sort of business her husband had been involved in. He got the impression that it may not have been legitimate, especially considering her companionship with Petrov. Although Falco had yet to prove the Russian was a thief and smuggler.

"Then you intend to travel beyond Shanghai?" Falco asked.

"No," Petrov said with a shake of his head. "Shanghai. We have liquor to sell. What better place than Shanghai?"

"Do you live in Shanghai, Mr. Falco?" Mie Lee asked.

"No. Hong Kong."

"Then you won't be traveling to Shanghai, only as far as Hong Kong?" There was a small disappointed turn of her lips.

Sister Catherine spoke up with exuberance. "Oh no, all the way to

Shanghai. John is taking me there to show me the city. Lots of clubs and entertainment."

Mie Lee looked at Sister Catherine with a warning gaze in her brown eyes. "But a very dangerous place, too, Mrs. Murdoch…Kate. You must be careful where you visit. I'm sure your brother will protect you. He seems very capable. But you do not seem one to indulge in the night life of Shanghai, Mr. Falco."

"John…please. I don't drink alcohol but I do enjoy jazz. There are some very good jazz clubs in Shanghai. Do you like jazz, Mrs. Lee?"

Her eyes grew shaded, her eyelids lowering slightly as she looked steadily at him. Her lips finally curved into a warm smile that defrosted her coolness.

"Please call me Mie. Yes, I do like jazz. Perhaps you would consider escorting me to some of these jazz clubs for an evening when we reach Shanghai."

Sister Catherine grinned and elbowed Falco in the ribs.

Mie looked quickly at her. "If I would not be intruding upon your visit, Kate."

"Not at all," Sister Catherine said. "I'm sure John would welcome your company over his older big sister all the time."

"That would be good," Petrov announced. "I have business I must do. Mrs. Lee does not like to be dragged everywhere when I do business. Very boring."

Mie moved a slender hand toward Petrov, flicking a long enameled nail at him. "Serge was a business partner of my husband. We continue to be business associates. I run Mr. Lee's companies. All very boring, indeed, but necessary. I like the wealth they provide."

Petrov raised his vodka glass in a solute to Mie Lee. "She is a very astute business person. It comes very naturally to her. If I may be so bold, Mrs. Lee is better businessman than Mr. Lee ever was."

Falco sipped his tea, which was bland and not hot. He imagined the ship's bar got very few requests for tea. When he glanced through the crowd, he saw one of the stocky Russians who had been with Petrov when he had arrived at the docks. He was nursing a mug of beer while watching their table. Falco caught his eyes and received a deadly stare in return.

Keeping an eye on Petrov might be easier but it did not solve the problem of examining the crates in the cargo hold. If Petrov and his bodyguards suspected him in any way, they would be keeping a close eye on him and a closer scrutiny on their crates. Perhaps he could alleviate any suspicion the Russian might have by playing up an attraction to his companion. The widow was pretty, only a few years older than him, and wealthy. Such an attraction would seem natural, though Falco wondered what this woman's business really was.

Returning to his cabin, Falco rubbed his eyes with both hands as though he were exhausted. He wasn't. He tried to control his thoughts. He needed to push his emotions aside, to find his balance. When he closed and locked the cabin door, he stared at it for a moment before turning to face the smiling woman.

"Sister Catherine," he began.

"You'd better get used to calling me Kate, John, if we are to keep up the pretense of being brother and sister in order to continue your investigation of Serge Petrov."

He took a deep breath. "Kate. I was trying to keep a low profile, to keep my distance and not raise Petrov's suspicions. If he had not noticed me he would not pay attention to me. Now I have not only him aware of me but Mrs. Lee and two bodyguards. I have no idea who else on board he might be associated with. I need to be even more careful."

She grinned wider and wagged her finger at him. "But now you can analyze him up close, ask him surreptitious questions about his business or his plans after disembarking at Shanghai, who his associates might be. Ask him about his cargo, like what kind of liquor he is transporting, how many bottles, where it's eventually going."

"And make him even more suspicious. I am not a merchant, club owner, bartender or even a drinker of alcohol, so it is none of my business. My only intention for being on board was to examine the cargo crates, not to interrogate Petrov."

She continued to smile at him. "Now you can do both."

"But I don't want to. I only need to know if he has stolen artifacts in those crates and pass that information on to the proper authorities. I have no need to interact with Petrov and his companion."

She flicked her wrist at him, nearly slapping his chest. "Oh, you like this spy thing, don't you? I saw the way you looked at Mie Lee. She's pretty, isn't she?"

"And obviously very dangerous. Her husband was a business partner with Petrov, and if he is a smuggler then Lee was involved in illegal activities. Mrs. Lee is continuing those activities. I'm hardly interested in a romantic relationship."

She winked at him. "But it wouldn't be out of the question."

His voice became more stern. "Sister Catherine, please leave my social life out of this. And do not drag me into any more social activities."

Her lips drew into a pout. "Oh, that wouldn't be suspicious, now would it? You meet a woman who has shown some interest in you, and you disappear into your cabin for the rest of the voyage."

"I don't like social events. I prefer to be by myself."

Sister Catherine crossed the deck to her bunk, eased herself down and slipped off one shoe. She massaged her bare foot with both hands, breathing out a sigh.

"Oh come now, Johnny. You don't go out on the town in Hong Kong? Don't you have friends?"

"Yes, I have friends." He felt as though he were defending himself against allegations of being a hermit at twenty-five. "And yes, I do go out occasionally to clubs. Well, one in particular. I happen to like jazz."

Her massaging fingers stopped and she looked up with incredulity in her wide eyes. "Really?"

"Yes. Why?"

"Oh, nothing. I just don't see you as a fan of jazz. Can't stand it myself. I just thought you were the type to appreciate classical music."

Falco wondered when this conversation slipped from being his attempt to reprimand Sister Catherine into her berating him for enjoying jazz.

Falco held up both hands. "I'm leaving so you can prepare for bed."

As he turned to the cabin door, she stood up, one foot bare, the other still in her flat shoe.

"You aren't going down in the hold, are you?"

"Not until very late. I already located Petrov's cargo but I was not able to search deep inside. I only found some bottles I suspect are liquor, as the manifest explains, but I cannot tell if contraband is buried deeper inside. I need more time in the cargo hold without being interrupted, so I will go down before sunrise."

She kicked off her other shoe. "Good. I'll go with you. Admit it, you need my help. I can watch to make sure the coast is clear."

He did not want to admit that this had been his plan but she was becoming a headache for him. If he was able to determine in this first night that the stolen temple articles were in at least one crate, he could have the captain of the ship lock Petrov in his cabin until they reached a British port, like Hong Kong. If he had to endure Sister Catherine's assistance to have a quick ending to this affair, then he could push back his trepidation concerning the woman.

"Very well. Try to get a little rest."

"What about you?" she asked as Falco unlocked the door.

He paused while facing the door before pulling it open. "I need a walk."

6

When Falco returned to the cabin, Sister Catherine was asleep in her bunk. He pulled off his jacket and tie and slipped out of his shoes. Since his nightly routine of exercising might disturb her, he opted instead to sit cross-legged on the wood deck and meditate. He needed to calm himself. The stroll along the deck had helped, but when he noticed the two Russian bodyguards he began shadowing them. They disappeared into the ship's hold, only to come back a few minutes later before Falco had a chance to follow them down a gangway. They spent the next hour leaning against the aft railing, smoking black cigarettes. Eventually they returned to their cabin.

Falco watched from outside. Lights shown through the portholes of Petrov's cabin and that of the two bodyguards. The cabin where Mie Lee stayed was dark. She appeared to have retired early.

From the sounds of glass upon glass, Falco at first thought Petrov was entertaining, but since there was no conversation he assumed the Russian was drinking alone. The sounds were consistent with a bottle tapping on the rim of a glass as the glass was filled over and over. When snoring drifted through the open porthole, he was certain Petrov was alone and now asleep. His bodyguards soon turned off their light. Since their porthole had remained closed, he could not hear their snores.

Falco waited until two hours before dawn to rouse Sister Catherine.

She sat up, wide awake.

"Is it time?" she asked, eyes wide and bright.

"Yes. Dress quickly. We'll go down into the cargo hold."

In less than a minute she was dressed in trousers and a knit pullover. He blond hair was tousled and roughly brushed. Falco had pulled on his shoes but left his jacket and tie, rolling back the cuffs of his shirt. His small flashlight he tucked in his back pocket.

Before heading into the bowels of the ship, they passed the upper deck where Petrov and his entourage had their cabins. Petrov's light was still on but his snores resonated through the night.

Even members of the crew were nowhere to be seen. The decks of the ship were deserted, any crew members up at this hour were part of the night shift and were at their posts.

Followed closely by Sister Catherine, Falco took gangways down into the bowels of the ship. Corridor lights were low, turned down for the night. They passed no crew members on the way. They moved aft, where the drumming sounds of the engines grew louder and the steady vibrations hummed through the deck plates. At a watertight hatch, he motioned Sister Catherine to stand against the bulkhead, then he spun the wheel to release the locking bolts. He slowly swung the hatch outward.

"I thought this was the cargo hold," Sister Catherine whispered against the loud throb of the engine and the blast of heat from the boilers.

Falco held his finger to his lips. "I need to borrow something first."

With another wave of his hand to keep her in place behind the opened hatch, Falco slipped inside the engine room.

Below, he could see a handful of crew with shovels, ready to keep up the level of coal in the boilers. The heat rising up to this higher level was intense, even at this distance. During the day, the heat must be unbearable. There were three brawny Chinese covered in perspiration, bare to the waist, leaning on shovels, and one grimy engineer watching gauges to the boiler. Dressed in his shirtsleeves, Falco could have been taken as one of the crew at a glance. No one paid him any attention as he walked to an equipment locker on this upper scaffolding, eased it open, and pulled out a foot long pry bar and a large, heavy flashlight. He checked the flashlight for power, shining it inside the locker. Its bright beam flashed. Satisfied, he tucked it under his arm and closed the locker.

Once back in the coolness of the corridor, he pushed shut the hatch and dogged the clamps into place. He handed Sister Catherine the flashlight, keeping the pry bar in his left hand. He motioned her back the way they had come.

Another watertight hatch led to the cargo hold. He turned the wheel, pulled open the hatch, and took his own small flashlight from his back pocket. Its slim beam stabbed through the black cavern of the hold.

"Where are Mister Petrov's crates?" Sister Catherine whispered.

"Further in."

"Let me turn this on," she said as she swung up her borrowed flashlight.

The blazing beam caught Falco in the eyes, blinding him. He shut his eyes against the burning glare, reached out, and gently pushed the flashlight down. When the spots began to fade from his eyes, he guided Sister Catherine into the hold and pulled shut the hatch, dogging it in place.

Motioning her to follow, he wound his way through the stacks of crates, boxes, bales and luggage until he came upon the familiar three crates under the cargo netting.

"These are the crates," he explained. "I need you to go back to watch the hatch in case someone comes in. You'll be able to hear the hatch unlock. There's another hatch on the other side but you won't be able to see it. You'll be able to hear it. If anyone starts to open either hatch, come and warn me."

"Will you be looking in the crates?"

"Yes. But I can't watch for anyone coming in at the same time."

She grinned. "That's why you need me."

Spinning around, she pranced along the stacks of cargo.

Falco climbed up the heavy netting, pry bar in one hand, flashlight in the other. Balance on the top crate, swaying with the movement of the ship, he unlashed the netting from the bulkhead, releasing enough of the net to be pulled away from the lid of the first crate. Moving off the lid, with his feet in the net, his left arm through the ropes, he was able to shove the edge of the pry bar under the lip of the lid. With a groan of wood, the lid lifted. The sound pierced the black hold like a scream.

Sister Catherine's flashlight beam danced through the hold.

"Is everything all right?" came her hesitant question.

"Yes," he hissed. "Go back and watch the hatch."

As the beam bounced back among the stacks, Falco eased the wooden lid up. He sent his light inside. Straw covered the contents. Pulling it aside, the beam glittered over the amber glass of a bottle. Moving away more straw, he exposed other bottles. Lifting the closest, he set it on top of others. Digging through the straw, he found another bottle. He tugged it free and placed it with the first. Then he shoved his hand deeper into the straw. His fingers touched something cold and smooth, but without the feel of glass. Exploring deeper, he felt contours and curves. It was smaller than a bottle. By stretching, with the edge of the crate digging into his armpit, he could encircle the object with his fingers. Tugging gently, he pulled it free of the straw bedding.

Balanced precariously on the edge of the second crate, as he used to perch for hours on a post on one foot during his time at the Shaolin temple, he lifted the object up and turned his flashlight in its direction. The white beam bounced off the smooth gold surface, showering the cargo hold in yellow.

The serene face of a five-inch tall Buddha looked calmly back at Falco. Either it was solid gold or had a thick covering of the precious metal.

7

Falco climbed down the cargo net to the deck, cradling the small gold Buddha statue. He set his pry bar down and lifted the little statue on his palm, shining his light over it. It was of Hindu design, not Chinese. He couldn't determine its age but it did not look very old. There were no markings on it, no Hindi or Chinese characters. It could very well have come from one of the temples in Singapore. There was no way to prove one way or the other.

"Ooh!" Sister Catherine breathed. "It's beautiful."

Falco spun on her. "Sister Catherine! Please watch the hatch."

"But it's one of the stolen artifacts, isn't it?"

"It might be."

The silence around them was disturbed by the grind of metal as the wheel on one of the hatches spun and it creaked open on its hinges.

Falco tucked the Buddha under his arm, reached out, and pushed the button to extinguish the Sister's light, turning his own flashlight off at the same time. Then he reached out in the darkness to pull her toward a pile of cargo.

Half of the lights suspended from the overhead girders blazed on.

Heavy footsteps sounded on the deck, coming toward them.

Falco shoved his flashlight into his back pocket and pushed Sister Catherine deeper into the space between stacks of crates, handing her the small gold statue.

The squat Russian bodyguard stormed through the canyon between piles of cargo and stared up at Petrov's violated property. Looking down, he saw the discarded pry bar, bent, and picked it up. He slapped it against his palm as he turned to gaze around the hold with rage written across his hard features.

Sister Catherine tried to squeeze further back, scraping her heel on the wood deck.

The Russian perking up his ears, then he struck.

He dove into the shadowy space where Falco and the Sister had hidden. He grabbed Falco by the front of his shirt, pulled him out, and swung the claw end of the pry bar at his head.

Falco ducked, the bar digging deep into a wooden crate beside him.

His fists shot up, his knuckles striking nerves in the Russian's arm. The pry bar fell loose and clattered to the deck. The Russian staggered back, then swung first his left, then his right fists at Falco.

Ducking each strike, Falco moved to block further punches. The Russian growled in anger and charged in an attempt to catch Falco to squeeze him to death.

Falco's right fist struck the Russian between the eyes, in the nose, then mouth, and finally in the center of his chest, all strikes so fast that the Russian could only blink at the speed. He stumbled back, shaking his head clear like a raging bull.

Sister Catherine stepped clear of the crates, hugging the gold statue.

The Russian's eyes went wide as he saw her holding the stolen piece. His dull mind put everything together.

In the brief pause, Falco struck. He was too close to his opponent to use his feet, but he stabbed with fingertips and knuckles, hitting pressure points. The bodyguard dropped to his knees. Then he roared and dove into Falco, broad shoulder shoving into Falco's stomach, pushing him into the stack of Petrov's crates.

Falco grunted as pain shot across his back.

The Russian pushed himself to his feet and wrapped his thick arms around Falco, squeezing. The air rushed from Falco's lungs and he tried to wiggle his arms free. He wrapped one leg around the Russian, but he had no leverage to do anything.

In a blur of shadows, he saw Sister Catherine hovering behind the Russian. She set down the gold figurine and picked up the discarded pry bar. She swung, and the Russian's deadly grip fell away.

Petrov's bodyguard dropped backward to the deck.

Sister Catherine stepped out of the way, dropping the pry bar, and staring in horror.

"Is … is he …"

Falco took in a deep breath and knelt, feeling the ache in his back and ribs. He did not see any blood, but there was a deep indentation in the Russian's temple. The pry bar had crushed his skull. There was no need to check for a pulse.

"He's dead."

Sister Catherine sucked in a breath. "Oh my God!" She made the sign of the cross, her face whiter than her normal paleness, her eyes bulging.

Falco picked up the pry bar and climbed up the cargo netting. After rearranging the bottles in their nest of straw, he pulled down the crate's lid and used the bar to hammer it back into place. Then he pulled the net up and lashed it once again to the bulkhead.

When he climbed down, Sister Catherine still stared at the dead body.

He took hold of her by the shoulders, turning her toward him.

"Sister Catherine. It wasn't your fault."

"But I killed a man!"

"You were trying to help me. It was an accident."

She crossed herself again, between his outstretched arms.

"What can we do?" she asked, looking up at him.

"I have to get rid of the body. If they discover it here, they'll know someone was examining the cargo. Can you return to the cabin on your own or do you need me to take you back?"

She took several deep breaths before looking at him again. This time her eyes were narrowed with determination.

"He's a big man. How are you going to take care of him yourself?"

"I'll manage."

She shook her head. "No. I did this. It's my fault. I must pay pennants for it. He was an evil man, a killer, but I still took his life from him. It wasn't for me to do. Vengeance belongs to the Lord. I must pay for this."

"You can make a confession when we reach Shanghai, Sister. Right now we need to get rid of the body."

"You mean throw him overboard?"

"Yes."

She pursed her lips and nodded. "May God forgive me."

He reached down and picked up the Buddha figure. "He's the forgiving sort, Sister. It's what He's famous for."

He handed it to her and she made a half attempt at a smile.

He found her flashlight and gave it and the pry bar to her. Then he reached down to tug on the Russian's limp arm, starting to lift him up.

Sister Catherine stared at the pry bar for a moment, then tucked it and the flashlight with the small Buddha under her arm and helped to shove the stocky Russian. Cradling the body between them, Falco dragged it toward the hatch and shoved it through.

Falco turned off the overhead lights and shut the hatch, spinning the wheel to lock it in place.

Dragging the body to the upper deck took time. They had to conceal themselves once in another corridor while a crewman went by. At the ship's aft, Falco searched and listened for any signs of wandering crew or passenger. They encountered no one else. Together, they shoved, pushed and nudged the Russian's lifeless hulk to the aft rail and thrust him into the churning wake of the ship. The sound of his splash was lost in the night and petulant sea.

Then Falco took the flashlight and pry bar from the sister. He paused, thought he should replace both to the equipment locker, but needed to get Sister Catherine back safely to their cabin. She looked relieved as he sent both light and murder weapon into the ocean.

Sister Catherine paced the small cabin, twisting her hands together. "This is terrible. What am I to do?"

Falco sat in one of the wooden chairs with the golden statue resting serenely in the center of the table in front of him. He wished he could have searched the crates for more evidence, but the Sister was too distraught. He wondered if the life-size gold Buddha from the Siong Lim Temple was in the bottom crate, which was large enough to hide it.

He looked up at Sister Catherine. "It was an accident. You didn't mean to do it."

She spun on him. "But I killed a man."

"He could have easily killed both of us. I may not have overpowered him." Falco was confident he could have turned the tables on the Russian, given enough time, but the Sister's intervention had put a quick end to the altercation. He wasn't about to point out that he had fought other opponents who were even larger and stronger. He didn't want her to feel any worse than she did. Best to let her believe she saved his life.

Sister Catherine gave him an apologetic look. "You were doing pretty good against him at first, but you are not a big man. I couldn't stand by and let him kill you. How did you learn all that fighting stuff?"

"From the Shaolin monks."

"Then you aren't Catholic?"

"No." His father was Catholic. That relationship did not endear him toward that belief.

"You're a Buddhist?" Her eyes widened incredulously.

"No. Well, not quite. I would be considered a monk by some. It's rather complicated."

Sister Catherine sank into the chair opposite. "So a monk and a nun kill a man. It sounds like a crude joke but it isn't funny. And a man is still dead. By my hands."

She looked up at him. "Did you ever kill anyone, Mr. Falco?"

He paused a moment to consider then said a soft "Yes." He paused again and added, "Even though it has been justified each time, it is not something you can easily get over. It takes time to deal with."

She nodded toward the little gold Buddha. "What are you going to do about that?"

Falco picked it up. It was heavy. If there were others in the crate, it would weigh more than what he could handle by himself. He could not get to the bottom crate on his own. Nor would Sister Catherine be able to help in that situation.

"I need to go to the captain. If his ship is carrying contraband, he would be liable. He would be anxious to take care of it, investigate the crates, and notify the proper authorities. I imagine he would keep Petrov under house arrest and turn him over to the Hong Kong police when we reach the port."

"Can we trust the captain?"

Falco shrugged. "I don't know him, but this is a reputable shipping line. He would need to obey maritime laws to the letter or loose his position. The sun's coming up. You get some rest before breakfast and I'll seek out the captain."

He stood up, taking a handkerchief from his inside pocket and wrapping it around the statue. Then he placed the artifact into his jacket's side pocket.

Sister Catherine stood also, her movements more urgent. "Oh, I'm afraid I couldn't rest at all. I'm all jitters. Can't I come along? I won't get in the way."

Falco immediately regretted his acquiescence, but Sister Catherine joined him on deck in the cool breeze of early morning, the sun bathing the ocean in crisp yellow. He headed for the bridge, feeling that either the ship's master would be there or that the crew would know his whereabouts.

Falco had previously seen the captain of the *Queen of Sumatra*. Hugo Nilsson was a large man in his fifties, thick beard turning gray, wavy black hair white along the sides and thinning on top. He kept his cap on whenever he was on duty, removing it only when he joined the passengers for dinner at the captain's table. From what Falco could learn, Nilsson was twenty years with the Straits Steamship Company, the last ten as a ship's master. Before that, he spent more than ten years on various steamers sailing the Pacific. There was little left of his native Swedish accent. Falco had passed him once on his wanderings through the steamship, as the captain was discussing ship's matters with two other officers. Falco had smelled the pungent odor of tobacco mixed with traces of alcohol. So Captain Nilsson enjoyed his cigar and a moderate amount of bandy.

"I saw Captain Nilsson at dinner last evening," Sister Catherine said as they climbed a gangway, heading toward the bridge. "Lovely man. A bit rough around the edges but he kept his humor in check since there were ladies present. I wasn't at his table, mind you. There seemed to be some wealthy passengers who were granted a place at the captain's table. Some Shanghai banker, a French businessman, and their wives. The wives were giggling all during the meal. Honestly, I think they were both flirting with him. He does cut a rather romantic looking figure, if you like that sort of thing. Of course, I don't. He may have been handsome in his youth but he has a few extra pounds around the middle and is a little past his prime."

Falco half listened as they neared the upper deck of the ship. Passengers would not be allowed on the bridge but Falco felt confident that he would be given an audience with the captain once he explained his connection with the Singapore police and the governor.

Captain Nilsson stood just outside the bridge, in earnest conversation with a passenger in a suit and hat. Falco paused before climbing the last gangway and watched. Sister Catherine bumped into him, then fell quiet as she too looked up toward the captain and his guest.

Petrov was in heated dialogue. The Russian spoke quickly in hushed tones that drifted away and could not be heard.

Then Petrov pulled an envelope from his jacket's inside pocket and passed it to Nilsson. The captain looked inside, his thumb skimming over the edges of a bundle of currency bills. Then, with a glance around him, he shoved the envelope into the pocket of his white uniform jacket.

Falco motioned Sister Catherine back down the steps. She stumbled and turned around.

Heavy footsteps sounded on the gangway.

"Ah! Miss Kate! Mr. Falco. Good morning. Up early I see."

Sister Catherine spun with a grin on her face. "Why Serge, good morning to you. We're always up at the crack of dawn. Good to get some fresh air. Those cabins can get a bit stuffy."

"Yes indeed."

The Russian looked at Falco, who nodded back at him. Falco sensed an uneasiness, as though Petrov were measuring him. The Russian's eyes were bleary, lined in red from his own evening of indulging in liquor in his cabin, but he was sharp and wide awake.

Sister Catherine pointed up the gangway. "Isn't the ship's bridge up there?"

Petrov glanced over his shoulder. "Yes. I had some business with the captain. One of my associates, Boris, has gone missing. His partner, Vladimir, hasn't seen him since he left their cabin about three in the morning. He went on deck for a smoke and never returned. We have not been able to find him anywhere on board. I fear that he might have slipped and fallen overboard. He did have a little too much vodka last night. The captain is performing a detailed search of the ship. With hope he will be found in some hold sleeping off his intoxication."

Sister Catherine bowed her head, her features serious and compassionate. "I pray that will be the case and that he did not fall overboard."

"I too, Miss Kate."

He looked again at Falco, then nodded. "Perhaps we will see you both at breakfast?"

Falco gave a slight bow in reply. "And hopefully you can give us good news concerning your associate."

"Hopefully." The Russian excused himself and headed aft.

8

Falco could not get close to the cargo area for another examination. Ever since Petrov's associate went missing, either the remaining bodyguard was always present or a member of the crew prowled the lower decks at all hours.

Given the scene between Petrov and the ship's captain, Falco could not trust any member of the crew. His best bet seemed to be waiting until they reached Hong Kong when he could get in touch with authorities there. He had the one gold statue. If it could be identified as one of the stolen pieces it would provide evidence to have the rest of the cargo examined.

Which created the dilemma of what to do with the little Buddha. If it was found in his possession, it would ruin his plan and put both him and the good Sister in mortal danger. If the captain himself was bribed by Petrov then none of the crew could be trusted. Falco could not very well stay in his cabin until Hong Kong in order to watch over the little Buddha. He had to conceal it somewhere.

While Sister Catherine was out for breakfast, he removed the lowest drawer of the dresser. The furniture was built into the bulkhead and could not be moved. By the looks of the insides after the drawer was taken out, it had never been cleaned underneath. Wrapping the gold statue in a small hand towel, he tucked it inside and replaced the drawer, making certain it closed all the way.

Beyond that, he tried to keep to himself, reading and exercising while Sister Catherine took to the deck in search of entertainment and conversation.

"They want us to join them for dinner," she said after an afternoon stroll on deck.

Falco shook his head and closed the book he was reading. It was an older edition of a Margery Allingham mystery he had found in the ship's small library.

"I'll have something brought down."

"That won't work," she said. "It's been a whole day since I ... since we ..." She shook her head violently. "I don't know how I can keep facing them on my own. It was bad enough sharing breakfast and lunch with them, I don't think I can take any more of it. I'm bound to say something. Between Petrov and Mie Lee and now the captain involved, I can't trust anyone."

He nodded. "Okay. I'll join you." He doubted he could keep her from talking but at least he might be able to curb some of the conversation. He would have preferred her to not talk to Petrov at all, but she had already ruined the anonymity of the investigation. The best he could do was control some of the damage and not make the situation worse.

Dressed in his gray suit, he accompanied Sister Catherine to the dining hall. She wore a long red gown that clung to her thin figure, giving no suggestion at her true vocation. She even had a touch of makeup on her sallow face. Although she had been on deck, in the sun, for a few days, she had avoided too much exposure, wearing wide brim hats and seeking shade whenever she could. She had told Falco she did not tan but simply burned.

"You didn't pick that dress up at the convent," he observed.

She gave an embarrassed smile. "I bought it in Singapore with some other clothes when I thought of following you with your investigation. I wasn't sure it would fit. It seems a little tight. And I'm not used to my arms and back being exposed. I feel a little uncomfortable."

"It looks fine," he assured her.

The dining hall was already full of passengers with a mild rumble of conversation rising from their tables. All sorts of languages mingled into an incomprehensible blur of noise. Petrov, in a dark blue suit that look slightly less worn than his other clothes, stood up and motioned them to their table. He grinned at Sister Catherine, his eyes flashing up and down her. Obviously he approved of her choice of evening gown.

Mie Lee stood up, nodded at Sister Catherine, but held out her hand for Falco, smiling at him. She wore a gold colored gown of European design, her black hair curled in the latest fashion.

"You haven't been avoiding me, have you, Mr. Falco?"

He shook his head as he took her hand. "No, Mrs. Lee. I have been doing some reading."

She pouted as she sat. "I should feel insulted that a book has your attention instead of me."

He pulled out a chair for Sister Catherine. "I usually stay in my cabin whenever I sail."

Sister Catherine laughed, with just a trace of anxiousness. "He's always been like that. A wall flower. I could never get him to go anywhere."

"Yet he has moved to China," Petrov pointed out.

"Yes," Sister Catherine said, a little more serious. "Our roles have reversed, especially after I lost my husband. He has been trying to get me out of my shell, but he still likes to keep to himself."

"I must say," Petrov began, "there is not much of a family resemblance. You are very blonde and your skin is light. Mr. Falco is dark."

Sister Catherine patted Falco's arm. "We got that all the time, all our lives, haven't we, Johnny? I take more after our mother, Johnny after our father. Right, Johnny?"

Mie Lee looked at the Russian. "Serge, don't forget that John has spent many years in the Orient. Miss Kate has only recently arrived. Even *you* do not look like you did when I first saw you three years ago."

"Were you in Russia during the revolution?" Falco asked. He didn't like the conversation centering around him and the fictitious relationship with Sister Catherine. He needed to steer the talk elsewhere.

"No, I was in South Africa. It was over by the time I returned. The business I had represented had been owned by a rich industrialist. Now it is run by the proletariat."

"Is that better?" Falco asked.

"Much…it's fair."

A waiter came to take their order. Petrov ordered a healthy helping of steak and potatoes, both ladies going with fish, and Falco garnered looks when he asked for vegetables and fresh greens.

"You do not wish a juicy steak?" Petrov asked when the waiter left.

Falco shook his head. "I don't eat meat."

"What is the word?" the Russian said, searching for it.

"Vegetarian," Mie Lee put in. She smiled at Falco. "I don't blame you. Sometimes I want to abstain from meat. I rarely eat it myself anymore, though I love fish."

Fortunately the conversation drifted to other subjects and away from Falco's heritage and past. He still felt Petrov's scrutiny and expected some deeper questions at any moment that he could not answer.

When dinner came to an end, they said their good-nights. Petrov had invited them to the bar for a drink, but Falco graciously declined. Sister Catherine also made her apologies.

As Falco led the way through the passageways, Sister Catherine regaled about the evening.

"It was a little rough at first. Those questions about us being related. I mean, I think we handled everything well, but Serge seemed very suspicious. Do you think we convinced him? He is right. We don't look much alike. Maybe I should have posed as a cousin instead of a sister. But then I am a Sister, so maybe it was meant to be."

Falco unlocked and opened the door.

Sister Catherine fell silent when they looked at the small cabin littered with clothes and other articles. The room had been ransacked with no attempt to hide the search. Falco glanced at the dresser and saw the drawers opened and empty of their contents. The drawers had not been pulled free. He felt certain the searcher had not found the gold Buddha statue. He knew that had been their objective. Petrov's bodyguard had been deployed to find some evidence that Falco had searched his cargo and rid him of his one associate. The Russian's suspicions had been aroused and would not be easily quenched.

The morning the *Queen of Sumatra* steamed into Victoria Harbor, a cold drizzle filled the air. In the distance, hulls of military ships were lost in the gray air, looking like ghosts of battleships. Junks and sampans dashed out of the way as tugs guided the steamship to dock.

Falco leaned on the damp railing, hat shading his face. He looked up at the hills above Hong Kong, toward Victoria Peek. Through the fog and gray haze, he couldn't see the peek let alone the house of his friend Mzoma. That moderately sized mansion, owned by the Zulu prince, was his home, shared by Mzoma and their friend, Travis Flanagan, a former IRA terrorist. Falco had not been able to cable them of his arrival. He couldn't trust anyone on board.

Beside him, Sister Catherine stood sheltered under an umbrella. It was a heavy British affair, not a paper parasol favored in the Orient. It had been stashed in her trunk. She wore her khaki skirt and jacket.

"I've never been to Hong Kong," she said.

Falco eased himself straight. "With any luck, we can end this and there won't be any need to continue on this voyage."

She made a pout. "Oh, I was so looking forward to seeing Shanghai. I've heard so much about it. Is it really such a den of inequity? I heard it was the Paris of the East."

He turned toward her. "Have you ever been to Paris?"

She shook her head. "No."

"The comparison is accurate but Shanghai is much more. Besides the French Concession there is the International Settlement and the Chinese quarter. There are the clubs and gambling houses. Organized crime is rampant. Death is a very common occurrence. With the tensions between the Japanese and the Chinese, it is a very dangerous city."

"Are you going to the authorities here in Hong Kong?"

Falco nodded. "As soon as we dock. It won't be a long layover. Some passengers are only going as far as Hong Kong and maybe some of the cargo, but it's primarily for refueling, taking on more coal and supplies. We can slip off and I can pay a visit to a friend of mine. He'll get the ball rolling to have those crates investigated." He patted his coat pocket. The little gold Buddha statue rested inside, wrapped in a handkerchief. "We have evidence of contraband. The police will search for more. Petrov won't make it to Shanghai."

Further down the walkway he saw Petrov and his remaining bodyguard, accompanied by Mie Lee who had a red bamboo parasol decorated with dragons. The woman tilted back the parasol, saw him and flashed him a big smile with a wave of her dancing fingers.

Falco nodded in reply.

"Are you packed?" he asked Sister Catherine.

"Yes. Are we taking our luggage now?"

"No. We can have it picked up later, before the ship sails in the morning. I don't want to arouse Petrov's suspicions any more than they are."

Petrov and Mie Lee approached and the Russian put on a vague smile that did not reach his eyes.

"You won't be leaving us here, will you?" he asked Sister Catherine.

"No." She grinned, her eyes crinkling. "John is going to show me where he lives. Where is it you said? On Victoria Peek?"

Mie Lee raised her eyebrows in appreciation. "The Peek? There are some rather large homes up there. I am impressed, Mr. Falco."

"The house is owned by a friend of mine," Falco explained.

"Then you will continue on with us to Shanghai?" Mie Lee asked Falco. "You did promise to take me to some of the clubs to hear that jazz music you like so much."

He gave her a genuine smile. "Yes, Mie. The Jade Palace. I think you'll like it. Will you be visiting Hong Kong while we dock?"

"I will," she replied. "I want to do some shopping and have some Chinese food for lunch. The ship does not offer Chinese food and I miss it. Will you join me, John?"

"I'm afraid I won't be able to. I have some business to take care of before the ship leaves."

She pursed her lips in disappointment. "Another time, then. But you will be all mine when we reach Shanghai."

Sister Catherine looked to Petrov. "Will you be going ashore with Mie, Serge?"

"No. I stay. I will see all of you later."

Below, sailors tied off the lines to the dock and the gangway was lowered for passengers to disembark. Rickshaws waited, canopies keeping their seats relatively dry while their pullers were soaked through, hair plastered, clothes dripping. Passengers braved the drizzle to hurry down the gangway and take advantage of the waiting rickshaws or taxis.

Falco led Sister Catherine to the lower deck, then to the dock.

Falco flagged a taxi and told the driver to take them to the Hong Kong

Central Police Station. The cab deposited them in front of the station, a stone block building on top of a hill. The complex, dating back to the mid 1800s, included the Central Magistracy and Victoria Prison.

At the station's front desk, Falco made his request to see Detective Inspector Graham Hill. The Sikh desk sergeant picked up his telephone, spoke into it, then motioned over a Sikh constable, who conducted them through the maze of corridors to an office.

The tall, slender DI with a thick bushy mustache waved them in as he filled in reports. The constable closed the door and Sister Catherine sat in one of the wooden chairs in front of Hill's desk. Falco tugged the statue from his pocket, unwrapped it, and set it on top of Hill's paperwork.

The inspector looked at it, his pen paused. Then he set his pen down, studied the statue from all angles with a furrowed brow. He finally looked questioningly at Falco standing over him.

"We believe this was stolen from a temple and was being shipped to Shanghai with others," Falco explained.

"We?" Hill asked.

"This is Sister Catherine."

Hill reached out his hand. "Sister?"

Sister Catherine took his hand. "I know, I'm out of uniform. On temporary assignment, shall we say? Just call me Kate Murdoch."

Falco sat down in the other chair in front of the desk and launched into the story of his Singapore visit, the death of Colonel Eustace Butler, and the meeting with Sir Cecil Clementi and Harold Fairburn. Hill sat quietly with hands folded on the desk and listened without interruption. When Falco finished with his suspicions of Serge Petrov and finding the gold statue in his crate of liquor, Hill picked up the statue and turned it over in his hands.

"And there are more of these in those crates?" the inspector asked.

"I can't be certain. I was interrupted before I could make a proper search and since then Petrov has been very suspicious. I believe the larger crate has the Buddha of Monk Shi."

"Is that …" Hill began, then became very contemplative, sitting back and rubbing his chin with one large hand.

He finally leaned forward again and wagged a finger in the air.

"We'll get the harbor authority involved with this. They can examine cargo for contraband. Did this Petrov leave the ship?"

"As far as I know he's staying on board."

Hill pushed himself up. "Okay, you two stay away from the ship. I'll get a team of port authority inspectors and we'll go through the cargo. We'll use the excuse of looking for opium. You two stay clear. Can I reach you at Mzoma's home?"

"Yes," Falco said as he stood.

Hill lifted the gold Buddha statue. "I'll have this photographed and I'll wire Singapore to see if this is among the stolen pieces. We can add it to the others if we uncover a cache in those crates."

Falco helped Sister Catherine to her feet and escorted her from the office.

"So that's it?" she asked when they returned to the gray morning drizzle. "It's over?"

Falco smiled and hailed a rickshaw. "It soon will be."

He felt lighter, pleased he could bring this affair to an end without having to travel all the way to Shanghai. He was happy to be rid of the little Buddha statue and soon the gold Buddha of Brother Shi would be on its way back to Singapore. He did not relish another ocean voyage but he needed to accompany Monk Shi's Buddha back to the Siong Lim Temple to present it to the abbot himself. He didn't want anything else happening to it.

"Now what?" Sister Catherine asked as they squeezed into the rickshaw.

"Home. We'll see if Mrs. Wu would be kind enough to prepare lunch."

The rickshaw took them to Garden Road, where they boarded the tram to Victoria Peek. At the Peek Terminus, they took another rickshaw.

Mzoma's modest home had been the mansion of a French banker who had fallen on hard times at the start of the economic trouble. Mzoma's family owned diamond mines in South Africa and since he was one of the younger princes among many, he had no obligations to stay in Africa. After school in England, he traveled the world, eventually settling in Hong Kong. Sister Catherine stared at the house overlooking Victoria Harbor.

"This is your home?" she asked.

Falco paid the puller and guided Sister Catherine up the steps to the front door. "No. Mzoma owns it. I just live here. I helped Mzoma a couple of years ago and he insists I stay here. Travis Flanagan also lives here."

As he opened the door, a small Chinese woman in her forties came down the hallway, wiping her hands on a dish towel.

"Mister Falco, you back?"

"Hello, Mrs. Wu. Yes, I'm back and I've brought a guest. This is Sister Catherine. Sister, Mrs. Wu. She is Mzoma's housekeeper and cook."

Mrs. Wu furrowed her brow and shook the towel at Falco. "You no tell me you have sister, Mr. Falco. She not look like you."

"She's not my sister."

"You just tell me!"

"No, she's a Sister, a nun. With the Catholic Church."

Mrs. Wu eyed her suspiciously. "Don't nuns wear those funny clothes?"

Sister Catherine laughed. "Sometimes they let us wear regular clothes."

"Oh." Mrs. Wu nodded slowly. "Lunch ready in hour. Mister Mzoma in front room. I make ready guest room. Mister Flanagan still sleeping. Up late."

As Mrs. Wu trotted up the wide staircase, Falco whispered to Sister Catherine. "Her English is improving. She refuses to speak Chinese around Mzoma. His Chinese isn't the best."

A deep vibrato sounded to the left, with a slight British accent. "According to Mrs. Wu, my Chinese is atrocious, an insult to her ancestors. Hello. I thought I heard the front door. Welcome back, John. I'm sure Singapore proved interesting."

"Sister Catherine, may I present Mzoma."

Falco motioned to the tall, dark figure standing in the doorway. His head of close cropped black hair nearly touched the top of the door frame. He was tall, lean, with broad shoulders and a muscular frame dressed in a three-piece suit from London's Savile Row. At about thirty, he is a handsome man with smooth mahogany skin, a genial smile and bright brown eyes. He reached out his huge hand and engulfed hers in a gentle grip and gave a slight bow.

"A pleasure, Sister Catherine."

She looked up at the man towering over her. "Please, call me Kate."

"Then, Kate, come into the parlor and relax." Mzoma stepped aside and pulled out his pocket watch on it's gold chain. "Lunch will not be for an hour. Do you think that's long enough to tell us all the details, John?"

Falco gave a brief description of the events in Singapore and their eventual cruise toward Shanghai, with the stopover in Hong Kong. Sister Catherine added details, often interrupting to put in her involvement. Falco was not going to mention the death of the bodyguard, not wanting to upset Sister Catherine, but she described the details and her regret at the death.

Mzoma listened intently, not saying a word. When the narrative came to an end, he said, "Then it will be done this afternoon with the search for contraband. You will not have to go on to Shanghai but I suspect you will need to return to Singapore. Will you also return to Singapore, Sister Catherine?"

"I suppose so. I'll have to get back to my work with the locals."

Mrs. Wu came to tell them that lunch was ready. After eating in the vast dining room, they returned to the front sitting room.

No sooner had they settled than a knock sounded at the front door.

Falco shewed Mrs. Wu back to the kitchen, where she had been busy cleaning up the dishes from lunch. He opened the door for Graham Hill.

The inspector's face was grim as Falco escorted him into the sitting room.

Hill shook his head as he sat in one of the wing-back chairs. "Not good, John. I went with the port authority people, along with some of my own officers. Nothing."

Falco stared at him. "What do you mean?"

"We found those crates you told me about. Three crates for Serge Petrov. They weren't the only ones examined, since we didn't want to expose our hand. But when we came to those, all we found were liquor bottles in straw. In all three crates. It was unusual, because what were in the three crates could have been packed into one, but that wasn't an issue. We found no stolen artifacts and nothing had been off-loaded."

Falco shook his head. "That can't be right. I found that statue I gave you in the top crate."

"It was half full with bottles in straw."

"When I opened it, it was full to the lid. Petrov must have taken the temple articles out before you arrived."

Hill tugged on the corner of his drooping mustache. "I suspected he had, but I would have needed to open every crate on board. As it was, we did examine nearly all. Nothing. With the exception of some opium, which was impounded and the owner was arrested. It wasn't Petrov."

Sister Catherine leaned forward. "What could have happened to the stolen things? Do you think the captain hid everything?"

"They do seem to be in league with each other," Falco admitted.

"Did someone warn Serge?" she asked.

"Or he was expecting something when they sailed into Hong Kong," Falco suggested.

Hill eased himself to his feet. "Whether they were warned or not, it doesn't matter. Nothing was found. I'm sorry, John."

Falco sighed. "Looks like I'll be continuing on to Shanghai on the *Queen of Sumatra*. I'll need to see what happens when he unloads those crates. If the rest of the stolen pieces are hidden elsewhere, they need to either be replaced or somehow removed when they reach Shanghai. I need to find out where they are, particularly the Buddha of Monk Shi."

"I'll go back to the ship, too," Sister Catherine said.

"No." Falco shook his head emphatically. "Too dangerous. You can stay here. I'll have your trunk sent from the boat."

"No you won't. How suspicious will that look? I have to be there with you, Mr. Falco."

He didn't want her along. He realized that, at the moment, there was no arguing with her. He still had time before the ship sailed to convince her. He did not want her in a position of danger and he also did not want her interfering.

***

Falco hadn't seen the new passengers until the morning when he came out on deck, letting Sister Catherine sleep in.

The *Queen of Sumatra* prepared for departure. Lines were cast off from the dock. Engines pulled her into the bay and two tugs guided her out through the maze of junks and sampans. The sun tried to peek out through the heavy clouds. At least the rain had faded away, leaving Hong Kong damp and smelling fresher.

On the upper deck near the fore of the ship, Falco watched the tugs bring the ship into open water. He felt his skin prickle. Looking around, he saw a European in a brown suit staring at him. He was a blond man with a scar on his left cheek, his eyes cold. He was tall and broad, in his forties. His arms looked thick and muscular, but his belly had begun to expand. Falco hadn't seen him on the trip from Singapore.

Nor had he seen the two Chinese men in Western clothes on the lower deck who were looking up at him, whispering to each other. One was stocky, with a round face and gnarled, scarred hands. His companion was thinner and taller, but with the same snarl to his lips. Both in their thirties.

Falco wondered what other passengers were picked up in Hong Kong.

Petrov strolled onto the upper deck and the European with the scar gave him an imperceptible nod, turned, and left the deck. Vladimir stood in the distance, keeping an eye on his employer.

"Ah, Mr. Falco," Petrov called as he approached. A smile creased his face. "So good you haven't left us yet. I was afraid you might have stayed in Hong Kong."

Falco suspected that either his minions or members of the crew had stolen into his cabin while he was gone and had seen the packed trunk of Sister Catherine and his own small bag. Maybe that had made Petrov more suspicious than he already was and had caused him to remove the temple artifacts from his crates. Somehow Falco didn't think so. He wouldn't have had enough time before the inspectors from port authority arrived. They had already been moved. They were expecting to be searched.

"I had promised my sister to show her Shanghai," he told the Russian.

"And Mie Lee is looking forward to spending some time with you in Shanghai," Petrov said as he leaned on the rail beside Falco. "She is quite taken with you."

"She honors me."

Petrov turned and looked at Falco. "You sound like a Chinese. I think maybe you've been here too long."

"It's a wonderful, ancient culture."

The Russian shrugged. "Perhaps. But always at war, it seems. Between warlords and Communists and invaders. But whom am I to talk? We Europeans just came out of a war not so long ago. You are too young to have fought, but you remember, yes? Where were you during the war, Mr. Falco?"

"New York City."

"Such a big city. Why did you leave?"

"My father wanted me to join the family business."

"And you did not want to? Tell me, what is this business?"

"Murder, mostly. Intimidation. Drugs, gambling, prostitution. Anything illegal. You see, my father is the boss of one of the biggest mobs in New York."

Petrov's eyes widened briefly. "Really? You surprise me, Mr. Falco. I had no idea you were from such a family."

"I didn't want any part of it. I left when I was quite young. Haven't been back since."

The Russian slowly nodded. "No stomach for such a violent life. I understand. I have been in war. There was revolution in my country, though I was not there at the time. I have seen violence. I have committed violence when it was needed, but I abhor it. I would much rather that everyone is reasonable. You are a reasonable man, Mr. Falco. You would wish to avoid violence, am I right?"

Falco gave him a smile. "Whenever possible."

"Good! Then we understand each other."

Petrov pushed away from the railing. "I hope we see you at lunch. Mie Lee will be anxious to tell you about her visit to Hong Kong."

Falco watched as the Russian walked away, his thoughts revolving over the implied threat of his words. They amused him. As did Petrov's new associates, replacements for his missing Boris. Obviously he saw Falco as a great threat and intended to keep a close eye on him. Falco wondered how many other thugs he had picked up in Hong Kong. Did any of them know him? Were they associated with any of the local triads? He had a reputation as a troublemaker. Petrov might toss him overboard at some point during the voyage to Shanghai. Falco wasn't looking forward to a long swim back to Hong Kong.

9

Falco strolled the deck more often than he would have liked. He wanted to keep an eye on Petrov and his cronies as well as the crew. He was making a target of himself and he couldn't help feel he was doing it to temp fate. He should have stayed in his cabin as much as possible, which is what he was incline to do on ocean voyages. However, this trip was different. He was on a ship full of enemies.

On the second evening, he walked near the aft of the ship and found himself alone on a deck only illuminated by the quarter moon.

Footsteps sounded behind him.

Two sets, trying for stealth but doing a miserable job of it.

He let them sneak up on him, as though he were ignorant of their presence. He could smell their body odor over the salt air. In a moment, they would have their hands on him.

He spun, finding Petrov's two Chinese hoodlums, one with a piece of pipe in his thick hand. This was the one who was squat and heavy. He swung the pipe at Falco's head with the intention of braining him. Falco ducked into a crouch and the pipe tousled his hair at it passed overhead and slammed into the thinner Chinese right next to him.

The second man screamed and fell back against the railing, hands flying to his face and blood dripping from his bruised mouth and split lip.

The surprised assailant tried to swing his pipe again, but Falco's foot swept in a circle to catch the man's knee. With the pipe flying from his fingers, the man went down,. He rolled and got to his feet, growling like a buffalo. He stomped into a charge. Falco waited until he closed in, then ducked to the side and let the man stumble. The thug crashed to the deck, but got up in a rage. He swung his fists, which Falco easily avoided.

As the man tired, Falco swung his foot up and struck him on the side of his face. The man twisted into circles that caused him to collide with his thinner ailing partner.

Then the thinner man untangled himself and found the pipe as it rolled along the deck, picked it up, and swung at Falco.

Falco ducked out of the way each time the man swung, avoiding the pipe. The man's face became puzzled. Then his eyes widened as Falco's foot shot up and struck him hard on the side of the face. The man stumbled back against the railing, arms dropping to his side, and the pipe hanging loose in his fingers

The heavy set man, his face bleeding, crawled to his feet and charged with his fists up, but Falco twisted aside and the heavy thug bounced off the railing. His thick arms cut through the night air again, but his fists never connected. Falco easily blocked every punch. The man's anger boiled and he dove at Falco attempting to grab and encircle him to crush him. But Falco stepped slightly out of the way and the thug's arms caught only empty air. Left unbalanced, he tilted and toppled onto the railing.

The thinner man came swinging the pipe again. Instead of whacking Falco, who spiraled away, the pipe hit the back of his associate's head. The thug bent further over the rail. His partner grabbed at his ankles. With a grunt he lifted tumbled the heavier man over the railing.

The sound of his splash into the water was lost to the churning of the engines.

The thinner man tossed the pipe after him. If his partner could swim, there was a chance, slim though it was, that he could swim to the shore of China.

The surviving thug raised his hands, signaling surrender.

"Why did you do that?" Falco asked in Chinese.

The man spoke hesitantly. "You're name is Faw-ko?"

Falco nodded.

"You are the one they talk about. The white Shaolin. I have heard of you but I did not know it was you when we were hired."

"What's your name?" Falco asked.

The man bowed his head. "I am Xiang Yi, Master. Forgive me. If I had known it was you, I would have refused the job. They had said a name but I did not recognize it."

Xiang Yi dropped to his knees and touched his forehead to the deck.

Wary it might be a trick, Falco stepped toward the man and encircled a hand around Xiang Yi's left arm, lifting him up. Then he saw in the man's eyes that his regret was genuine.

"Xiang Yi, I won't hurt you, but you should see the ship's doctor. Let me take you to the infirmary."

He touched his finger to his swollen mouth and saw the blood on his fingertips from the split lip. He shook his head.

"No, Master. Let them believe that Quong Hin and I fought. They will discover that he is gone. I will not blame you. He was a bully anyway. We were not friends."

"You were hired by Petrov?"

"Yes, Master Faw-ko. I thought it was to just intimidate, maybe kill a white man. I did not know it was you, even when they said your name." He shrugged. "Times are hard. We starve. Forgive me."

"No need," Falco said.

"This Russian … this Petrov. He is your enemy?"

"This ship is full of enemies," Falco answered.

Xiang Yi tried to smile through his swollen lips. One front tooth looked crooked. "You have at least one friend on board now, Master."

The following evening, Falco and Sister Catherine dined with Petrov and Mie Lee, as they had since the ship left Hong Kong. Petrov was in an exceptional mood, laughing and telling jokes. Falco suspected the good humor was forced but he could not sense any animosity from the Russian. Mie Lee seemed more subdued, giving Falco furtive looks as she nibbled her food. She sipped her red wine and drank more than she normally did. When the meal was finished, Petrov insisted that they visit the bar for a drink before retiring for the evening.

Mie Lee wrapped both her arms around Falco's right arm and pulled him close as they followed Petrov and Sister Catherine.

"Go on ahead, Serge," Mie said, her voice light and slightly slurred from her wine. "I would like to spend some time with John."

The Russian chuckled. "Of course. It is a warm night filled with stars. Very romantic." He grinned as he opened the door for Sister Catherine.

The Sister gave Falco a quick look with raised eyebrows before she disappeared into the crowded room filled with the melody *Dream a Little Dream of Me* wafting from the piano.

Some of the music drifted into the night breeze as Falco let Mie Lee guide him toward the bow of the ship. In the darkness, they passed Xiang Yi, who kept his head down. The Russian bodyguard, Vladimir, smoked a black cigarette as he leaned against the starboard railing, and stared out to sea, ignoring them.

Toward the bow, with no one nearby, she drew him to the railing.

"Serge lost another of his people last night," she said, her voice low and husky.

"How careless of him," Falco replied. "He seems in a good mood about it."

"Oh, that? What is one more man he doesn't have to pay and he will find more whenever he needs them. The man was a Chinese, which he doesn't care about. The other Chinese said they fought and the man fell overboard. He was a drunk and a bully."

"Serge's employees seem to have a drinking problem."

"I don't believe the man. Neither does Serge. He wanted them to throw you overboard."

Falco looked into her dark eyes. There was a twinkle in them as though the stars were reflected.

"His plan didn't work out, did it?" Mie Lee asked. "Xiang Yi insists that he was attacked by Quong Hen, that they never approached you. I don't believe that."

"Really? What does Serge believe?" Falco asked.

She pursed her lips. "I don't know. He doesn't trust you, John. He thinks you work for the government."

"Which one?" Falco smirked. "We just came from Hong Kong, so there's the British colonial government. Then in Shanghai there's the French Concession and the International Settlement. There's half a dozen governments represented there. And the British Straits Settlement government in Singapore. How about China?"

"Which one doesn't matter—"

"And what do you think, Mie?" He tried to keep his tone light. She might have been head of a ruthless criminal organization, but at the moment he saw a vulnerable young woman.

She looked into his eyes for a time. "I think … I think you are not what you seem to be, yet you are what you appear to be."

He smiled and shook his head. "That doesn't make sense."

"You are an honest man. You have beliefs that you adhere to. You will not compromise. Like the things you eat and drink. You seem like a Buddhist sometimes. Yet you are deceptive. You are small compared to Serge, but I can feel those muscles under your jacket. You could break Serge in half even though he is a bull of a man. You do not speak about yourself very much, so that you will not have to lie… deceptive," she finished.

"So you don't trust me either," he said.

"On the contrary, I do. I trust you to be you."

"Will *you* throw me overboard?" he mocked.

She turned to look out at the black ocean but laid her cool hand over his on the rail. "No one will hurt you. This boat is filled with your enemies. At a moment, any of them would stab you, shoot you, or toss you overboard. But no one will."

"And why is that?"

She turned into him again and looked into his eyes. She leaned against him. He felt her slender body tremble. "Because I told Serge that they will not hurt you."

Gazing at her, his voice was a whisper. "Why?"

"Because I like you, John."

She frowned and turned away again, her hand slipping from over his. "Oh, I know you probably don't return my feelings, but I cannot let them harm you. Even if it jeopardizes the business arrangement I have with Serge. I'll deal with the consequences later. I cannot have them kill you."

"Thank you, Mie. That means I owe you my life."

She turned to look at him and laughed. "I have the feeling that I am saving the lives of Serge's other men and some of the crew. Maybe even Serge himself. You have been in China a while. Did you spend time at any of the temples?"

"Yes. The Shaolin Temple."

She hung her head down and chuckled. "Then you are a Shaolin priest."

Falco didn't say any more and for a time they stood against the railing. Finally she lifted her head up toward Falco.

"John, I want to hire you."

"For what? I'm not very good at business, even though I don't know what business you're in."

"It doesn't matter. If I hire you, if you are working for me, you won't be in any danger. I don't know how long I can keep Serge from you."

Falco rubbed his chin and pursed his lips. "Do I have to kill anyone?"

She laughed. "I'll hire you as a consultant. You can be a liaison with the British and Americans. And you can be my bodyguard."

"It doesn't look like you need guarding. Even Serge respects you."

"How long will that last? You are an honest man. I want you next to me, even if it is temporary."

Falco sighed. "I can't make any promises. I won't work for you but I will help you."

She smiled at him. "That is as good as a promise."

She moved closer, snuggling against him and he put his arm around her. He told himself it was to shield her from the chill of the night's ocean breeze.

10

As the *Queen of Sumatra* steamed into the Huangpu River toward Shanghai, Falco could tell something was not right.

At the rail beside him as they stood on the deck below the bridge, Sister Catherine breathed in the sea air with other passengers crowded the forward railing for their first sight of Shanghai. Many murmured with concern. There were more warships than there had been before. They had passed a huge aircraft carrier before entering the river. Now half a dozen battleships appeared, the majority flying the flag of the Rising Sun. The *Queen of Sumatra* seemed tiny in comparison to the carrier.

Sister Catherine stretched, then looked toward the city with its famous Bund and the buildings with classic architecture.

"Hum. I don't think that's supposed to be like that. Are those fires?"

In the distance beyond Shanghai, several columns of black smoke curled into the brilliant blue sky.

Two planes buzzed high over the city. There were flashes below, then a number of pops sounded.

"They're bombing the city!" Sister Catherine exclaimed.

"It seems further away than the International Settlement," Falco observed, squinting into the bright sunshine.

He was aware of someone approaching and caught the subtle scent of jasmine in the ocean breeze. There was the light touch of soft fingers on his shoulder and he moved to one side to allow room for Mie Lee to join them.

"It's in the Chinese quarters," Mie Lee said. Her face was pale, her eyes dark and hollow. "The Japanese are bombing the Chinese areas."

Falco put his arm around her shoulders. "What happened?"

"Captain Nilsson had gotten word but never told any of the passengers. There's been an incident. The Japanese have been baiting us. First they had Japanese Buddhist monks spew anti-Chinese speech. There was a riot and one of those monks was killed. Then a Chinese factory was burned down in retribution, killing some Chinese. The Japanese claimed they are acting to protect their citizens. They're bombing in retaliation for riots. Refugees are fleeing into the International Settlement. There's fighting on the outskirts of the city. It's awful."

"That's terrible!" Sister Catherine said, crossing herself.

"Serge is arguing with the captain," Mie continued. "All he cares about is his shipment. He's afraid he won't be able to get it inland."

"It's part of your business, too, isn't it?" Falco pointed out.

"It's complicated." Her small mouth drew into a straight line of annoyance.

"Shouldn't we sail somewhere else?" Sister Catherine asked.

Mie shook her head. "The French Concession and International Settlement are safe. That's where hundreds of homeless are fleeing to. This is the sort of thing I was hoping to avoid."

Falco looked down at her. "How do you mean?"

"Nothing… I shouldn't have said anything."

"Is it something to do with what Serge is shipping in those crates along with his bottles of liquor?" he asked.

She shot him a glare. For just a moment, he saw in her a woman who was dangerous. "So you do know about that." Her voice was low and her words tight.

"I know that Serge has stolen temple artifacts and is shipping them somewhere. Are you involved with it?"

She looked at the crowd of passengers around them at the railing. "This is not the place to discuss this. Best you forget ever knowing it."

He took her wrist and pulled her away. He led her down the passageway to his cabin, opened the door and guided her inside. Sister Catherine followed them in and closed the door. Her trunk and Falco's bag were packed and sitting near the door.

"Is this private enough?" he demanded.

She glared back at him. "You are not a policeman. It is not your matter."

"A good friend of mine was murdered because of those stolen pieces and I made a promise to bring one back to them, the Buddha of Monk Shi. Doesn't it bother you that Petrov has desecrated temples?"

She shook her head. "I am not a Buddhist."

"I'm not either," Sister Catherine said.

"So? Serge is a thief. What does it matter that a few gold statues or some gold cups go missing. The money is better used elsewhere."

"For what?" Falco asked.

"That does not concern you."

"It does! I told you I would help you. I meant it."

She looked at him for a time, her features softening. She studied the sincerity in his eyes and her anger faded.

"You would still help me?" she asked.

"As long as it doesn't compromise the promise I made to return the Buddha of Monk Shi."

"Is that the large statue? It isn't very beautiful, like some of the smaller ones, but it is worth a fortune."

"It needs to be returned," Falco insisted.

She tossed her head. "Very well. But our plans are ruined anyway with the fighting. If only we had been a week earlier."

"Why?" he asked. "Why do you need so much gold?"

"To buy an army," she explained.

"An army?" Sister Catherine echoed over Falco's shoulder.

Mie Lee took a steadying deep breath. "Serge's plan involved melting down the temple statues at a factory north of Shanghai. It was one my husband owned, now I own it. Those bombs you saw falling? That is where the factory is. In the middle of the fighting. There is no way that we can get the gold through Shanghai and to the factory, if it is still there."

They heard a sudden banging on the cabin door.

Petrov's bull voice rang out from the passageway. "Anyone there? Hello!"

Mie Lee grabbed Falco's arm. "Don't tell him you know these

things, please. He is very volatile. He wanted to have you killed when he only suspected you. I may not be able to control him or his men if he realizes how much you know."

Falco nodded, then glanced at Sister Catherine, who mimed zipping her lips closed.

Once the door was open, Petrov burst in like an untamed animal raging to escape its confines. His red face puffed as he paced the small cabin, feet stomping on the thin carpet of the deck. He cursed in mumbled Russian. His thick fingers clenched into fists, which he waved about as though searching for an opponent to throttle.

"Those fools!" he finally said in English, standing still. "Why do they pick now to fight war?"

"Serge," Mie Lee said in a soothing tone, "we will find a way to go on."

The Russian screwed his face into a scowl and threw a dismissive hand through the air. Sister Catherine ducked out of the way.

"I have made arrangements," he said. "Nilsson was at least a little help. But this fighting. It ruins our plans. I have to come up with new one. Our buyers, we are to meet them in Shanghai. How are they to get here? And our merchandise …"

He glanced at Falco and lowered his brow in a glare.

"We will work matters out, Serge," Mie said.

He snorted. "*Nyet*! We cannot get cargo into Shanghai and we cannot meet with clients."

"I have a warehouse here, Serge," Mie said, her voice still calm. "We can store the boxes there until we are ready."

He shook his head violently. "No. I have made arrangements. I will not store them in Shanghai. Shanghai may fall to Japanese. I cannot trust them. Nilsson says the International Settlement is safe, but Chinese districts are not. This warehouse of yours, where is it? And you are Chinese, so it is owned by a Chinese. No Chinese business is safe from the Japanese. They claim they are protecting their people and territory, taking advantage to either seize Chinese property or destroy it. Your warehouse may be gone or in possession of the Japanese, like your factory. Your factory is probably bombed to dust. If it is still there, we cannot get to it. How soon will that happen to this warehouse of yours? No. I have made arrangements, as I say. I hired a boat. Nilsson will unload cargo to this boat."

Mie pursed her lips. "Smugglers? You did not consult me in this matter."

Petrov puffed himself up. "There was no need to. The cargo is mine."

"You work for me, Serge."

"Do I? I thought we were partners in this adventure. I am wrong, yes?" He narrowed his eyes toward Falco.

Sister Catherine rubbed her hands together and grinned. "So … everything with your cargo is okay? Does that mean you'll be sailing somewhere else? Back to Hong Kong?"

Petrov took a deep, calming breath. "No. My cargo will stay in harbor. Until I can determine where it needs to go. I must stay in Shanghai in case our buyers are able to arrive."

Sister Catherine gave him a quizzical look with a tilt of the head. "It's liquor, isn't it? Couldn't you find another buyer? I mean, with all the clubs and bars in Shanghai, you should be able to find someone who would pay you well for imported liquor."

Petrov forced a smile. "It is more complicated than that. These buyers, they were made certain promises. If I go back on my word my reputation will be ruined. I will make many people very angry. But that is no concern of yours. It is mine and I would not have you worry about my problems. You must go into Shanghai with your brother, enjoy your visit despite the fighting outside. Stay in the International Settlement and all will be well. Perhaps we will see you there."

"Didn't Captain Nilsson tell you?" Mie asked with a smug lift to her eyebrows. "He keeps you informed, doesn't he? Or perhaps he didn't know I wired ahead. I arranged for rooms for all of us at the Fairmont Hotel on the Bund."

Petrov glanced from Falco to Sister Catherine to Mie Lee. "All of us? I do not understand."

Mie smiled at him without warmth. "I didn't have the opportunity to tell you. I hired Mr. Falco."

The Russian's jaw dropped. "You … hired him?"

"Yes. He is to protect me and my interests."

Petrov laughed. “I thought you were just making love to him.”

Mie’s face darkened and her hand shot out to slap him soundly across the face. “I will not be insulted —”

Petrov stood stunned for a moment, then he raised his open hand to return her attack.

Falco caught his wrist and pulled him off balance, kicked the back of his right knee, and brought him down, twisting him so that his arm was behind his head, elbow pointing to the ceiling, his face screwed into pain from Falco’s fingers digging into pressure points.

Falco bent close to Petrov’s face. “Never hit a lady.”

He released Petrov and stood back.

The Russian rose, rubbing his right wrist with his left hand. He squeezed his eyes shut and seemed to be taking his time to think matters over. His chest began to rumble. Then he broke into a loud laugh that shook him from head to toe. He laughed long and hard, tears filling his eyes. He towered over Falco and reached out to slap him on the shoulder.

“Is good!” Petrov said through his mirth. “Is good, little man. You are a worthy foe, but I do not think I should fight you. Come, we are friends, yes? We are all friends!”

He held out his hand toward Falco.

Falco looked at it, and then into the Russian’s grinning eyes. He took the hand and felt the pressure of squeezing fingers. He met them pressure to pressure and exerted a little more until he saw a little wince on Petrov’s lips.

The Russian nodded in appreciation and laughed again.

“Mie Lee,” he said turning to the woman, “you have found an excellent defender. Mr. Falco, welcome to our little family.”

Sister Catherine folded her arms across herself. “Does that include me, too?”

Mie Lee stepped over and wrapped her right arm around Sister Catherine’s left. “You are my companion. We will be like sisters.”

Her remark and the smile she gave him made Falco more nervous than Petrov’s bullying.

11

While the *Queen of Sumatra* sat in the Huangpu River, waiting for docking at a wharf, one of the many junks plying the waters slowed and pulled along her side. Falco, alone at the aft railing of the upper deck, watched beneath the brim of his hat. Most passengers were on the forward rails and on the side to the city of Shanghai. This side was deserted except for crew who received lines from the junk and lashed it to the hull of the ship. Petrov himself oversaw the transfer of cargo. Captain Nilsson came down, watched the Russian hurling unnecessary orders at his men, shook his head, and walked away. The ship's master glanced up before he went below and saw Falco, giving him a deadly glare before disappearing through a hatch.

The crane lifted crates from the cargo hold, swung them over one by one to lower them to the deck of the old junk. Chinese crew on board the smaller craft took the crates in hand and stored them below.

Falco took in every detail of the junk. It looked as though a strong wind would blow the craft apart or a heavy wave would break it into driftwood. Any metal was rusted. Paint was faded and chipped. The sails bore frays and tears. Lines were soiled and stained. Faded Chinese characters on the bow gave the simple name *Lotus*. No registration numbers or any other identification. The crew were rough looking, all wearing rags, some in worn sandals, some barefoot. The men and their clothing were filthy. Among them was a captain who could be distinguished from the others only because he was the one giving orders.

The crates that passed over from the *Queen* were not those containing Petrov's liquor. These were smaller, oblong rectangular boxes resembling coffins. They were five very heavy crates that took several men to lower them into the junk's dark hold.

When Falco returned to his cabin, he nooticed Sister Catherine's trunk wasgone. Sister Catherine sat in a chair, elbows on the table, her forehead resting on her clasped hands, in an attitude of prayer. Falco quietly closed the door and saw his own bag resting on the floor.

"A steward came for the luggage," Sister Catherine said, straightening, bringing her hands down. "He said it'll be delivered to the Fairmont but I figured you'd want to carry your own bag yourself. I don't know anything about Shanghai. Is the Fairmont a decent hotel?"

"One of the finest," Falco said, taking off his hat and tossing it onto his bunk. "Politicians and film stars stay there."

Sister Catherine's eyes widened in surprise. "Oh, well then, I suppose it will do." She made a small giggle at her joke. "I'm certainly not used to luxury. At the convent we had a tiny room about the size of a closet with a cot only slightly more comfortable than the floor. And then while I have been in service, I tend to stay in huts or tents. Do you think our rooms will have a bathtub?"

"Definitely. I've stayed there before. You'll have your own room with your own bath."

"Oh, my."

After a moment, she looked at him with a quizzical expression. "Will you notify the authorities to have the cargo examined again?"

Falco shook his head. "It won't do any good. The gold artifacts aren't on board. I saw them loaded onto a junk."

"Then you've lost them."

"Not yet. Petrov has to deliver them somewhere. I just hope I can catch up with them before they are melted down."

"Then I shall pray that you can find them." She looked at him with a lopsided grin. "Of course, Mrs. Lee can always help, right?"

"Maybe," he answered.

"You and her have become rather close, haven't you?"

Falco frowned. "Not in the way you mean."

"But you have been spending some time with her. She's very fond of you. You haven't —"

"Don't get too comfortable around Mie Lee," he warned with a glare. "She may be a very dangerous woman. She is involved with smuggling at the very least. There have been murders, remember? Eustace Butler and his four assassins."

"You think she's involved with the murders?"

"More likely Petrov. Just be careful around her."

"What a shame. She seems so nice," she added with a sad look.

Within the hour, the *Queen of Sumatra* docked into her berth and stewards were helping passengers find their way to the docks of Shanghai.

Passengers crowded the gangways to leave the ship.

Mie Lee, followed by Xiang Yi, came to Falco's cabin.

"Our trunks are being sent to the Fairmont," Mie said as she entered, Xiang Yi waiting in the passageway. "Our rooms will be ready when we arrive. And we have reserved a taxi cab. Whenever you are ready …"

Sister Catherine jumped to her feet. "I'm ready! I appreciate being able to share this cabin but it has become a little claustrophobic. Perhaps I am not meant for ocean voyages."

"Nonsense, Kate," Mie said in encouragement. "You have done fine. You have not experienced any seasickness. That is half the battle."

"What about Mr. Petrov?" Sister Catherine asked. "Will he be joining us?"

Mie gave a smirk. "He and the captain have some business. He may join us later."

Falco lifted his leather bag and slung the strap over his shoulder. He stood aside and allowed Mie Lee through the door first, followed by Sister Catherine. In the passageway, Xiang Yi gave him a bow of his head and trailed behind him.

"May I carry your bag, Master," Xiang Yi asked in a low voice in Chinese.

"It's all right, Xiang Yi, but thank you."

They wormed their way among passengers and crew until they walked down the gangway to the docks bellow.

Half a dozen British soldiers stood on either side of the gangway, scrutinizing everyone who came down. An officer asked for papers and studied each passport. Sikh constables patrolled along the docks, hands resting on their sidearms. A scene that was normally filled with excitement was somber from the excessive military presence. Armored vehicles and military trucks from different nations rolled down the Bund, more prominent than European and American automobiles.

Xiang Yi scurried ahead of them and led the way to a line of four taxis waiting among a cluster of rickshaws. He anxiously pointed to the first taxi and hurriedly opened the rear door for Mie Lee. Once she was settled into the back seat, he raced to the other side and waved Sister Catherine to the door he held open. She slid to the middle of the seat, making room for Falco. Once he was in, Xiang Yi closed the door and the taxi took off.

Falco had expected Xiang Yi to take the seat next to the driver, but instead he disappeared among the crowd of passengers disembarking and trying to get a rickshaw or taxi under the watchful eyes of soldiers and police.

Smoke from burning buildings in the Chinese sections drifted over the tall European-style structures. Along the broad street, refugees carrying heavy bundles or pulling overladen carts sought a safe place to rest. Soldiers motioned them along. In the distance, the sound of rifle fire echoed through the streets of Shanghai.

Two Japanese biplanes flew overhead after their afternoon bombing run, heading for the aircraft carrier sitting in open water.

At the Fairmont, a uniformed doorman opened the rear door of the taxi. He was Chinese, wearing a fancy blue European-style uniform, and bowed as Mie Lee climbed from the rear seat.

On the opposite side, Falco got out and offered a hand to Sister Catherine.

When she stood on the street, with automobiles and military trucks rolling by, she looked up at the hotel towering over them. "Oh my!"

Falco guided her to the sidewalk. The doorman led the way, warning the crowd of displaced, homeless Chinese aside.

In the vast lobby of the Fairmont, Sister Catherine slowed and stared in awe around her, at the guests and staff and pillars and chandeliers. Falco tried to hurry her along to follow Mie Lee, who marched toward the desk without a glance at her surroundings. They caught up with her as the manager looked up from his paperwork and noticed her.

"Mrs. Lee! Welcome. It has been a while, hasn't it?" He greeted her with a French accent.

"Thank you, Claude," she returned. "How are your children?"

"Getting big. I sent them both to university in England." He lowered his voice and leaned closer to her. "It is no longer safe in many parts of the world."

She nodded in agreement. "We have reservations, Claude."

"Of course, Madame. I made them myself. The best rooms. As always. Your luggage has just arrived from the docks."

"You are such a dear, Claude. Thank you."

A bellhop, a young Chinese boy no more than fifteen, appeared beside the desk and Claude handed over three keys for the forth floor. He gave the boy instructions, then wished Mie Lee a pleasant stay.

The bellhop guided them to a closed elevator, gave the floor number to the operator, and rose to the forth floor with them.

On the forth floor, he stopped at one door, unlocked it, and stood aside.

Mie Lee passed him some coins and she was met at the door by a Chinese woman in a European maid's uniform who bowed.

"Mistress," she said in Chinese, "I have been unpacking your things. I will draw you a bath." She was probably a few years older than Mie but no more than mid thirties. Her accent was a bit odd to Falco, a mixture of different dialects. He couldn't place it.

"Thank you, Hua-ling." With a glance to Falco, she said, "I had wired Hua-ling to come to Shanghai and wait for me." She turned to the bellhop and took her key, asking, "Where are the rooms for the gentleman and the lady?"

The boy pointed across the hall and indicated the rooms.

"Is Serge's room along here too?" Sister Catherine asked.

"Heavens no," Mie exclaimed. "He is on another floor, in a much smaller room. All during the voyage from Singapore, his incessant snoring kept me awake. And he thought he could visit me whenever he wanted. I do not want him barging in on me at all hours." She gave Falco a small smile before she closed the door.

The bellhop went to the door, one down across the hallway. He unlocked it and motioned in. "For Madame," he said, trying to put a

French accent over his thick Cantonese one.

Sister Catherine elbowed Falco in the side. “I noticed your room is directly across from Mie Lee.”

Falco was grateful to finally lock the door to his own room. In the silence and solitude, he stripped down to his boxers and began rigorous exercises that he had been too light on of late. Within moments he was covered in perspiration and his mind was centered on the problem of finding the stolen temple gold, particularly the Buddha of Monk Shi. He could not fail to return that to the Siong Lim Temple.

12

They took lunch at the hotel's dining room, among the square pillars and the bright paneling, under white chandeliers. The crowd of guests ate quietly, the mood somber. The room was only half full, far fewer guests than Falco had seen in previous visits. They were richly dressed and Sister Catherine thought she recognized a film star from America, but Falco didn't know the name and had seen so few films in his time that he wouldn't have a clue. Some deference was shown to Mie Lee and her guests, as though she were a movie star herself. Obviously she had notoriety because of her more legitimate business concerns, handed down from her husband.

After lunch, she insisted on taking Sister Catherine shopping. Mie did not appreciate the Sister's fashion sense and insisted on helping to find clothes that were more up-to-date and fashionable in European circles.

"After all," Mie Lee explained, "you are now my traveling companion. We shall be seen in the finest places of Shanghai and Nanking. I cannot have you dressing like a school teacher. You must be fashionable. Only the best."

Falco declined to accompany them and they left the Fairmont, trailed by Mie's maid, Hua-ling, taking a taxi through the mass of wandering refugees.

Falco called for a rickshaw and headed in the other direction, to the Central Police Station on Foochow Road.

The headquarters of the Shanghai Municipal Police was busy,

people shouting in several languages, both officers and visitors from a variety of ethnic backgrounds. Some Chinese carried what remained of their worldly possessions in bundles. Japanese officers were rude and arrogant, which was returned to them in kind in Chinese, with Sikh and British police trying to keep peace.

Falco managed to find a Sikh not occupied with any argument and asked to see William Ewart Fairbairn. The Sikh recognized him in a moment and motioned him to follow him down a hallway to an office.

The tall, gaunt man in his forties, with short gray hair, round spectacles, and a face showing the souvenirs of countless street fights, stood behind his desk and greeted Falco warmly with a smile and a fierce handshake.

"What trouble have you brought to Shanghai this time, John?"

"Looking for a killer who has stolen temple artifacts," Falco said as he sat in the wooden chair in front of the desk.

He launched into his story, prefacing it with Butler's murder and the Governor of the Straits Settlements asking for his assistance.

"So this Russian, Petrov, is now in Shanghai?" Fairbairn asked when Falco had finished his severely edited version.

"He's on the *Queen of Sumatra*. His cargo was transferred to a junk with the name *Lotus*."

Fairbairn shook his head. "Not much help there. Probably a dozen junks with that name. This woman, Lee, she's involved with Petrov?"

"In a business sense."

"A business of theft and smuggling. Can you get more information from her?"

"A little at a time. I'm gaining her confidence. She may be the only way I can find out what will happen to that contraband. It was supposed to go to a factory she owns in Shanghai, but it's in an area that has been bombed. The factory may not be there any more."

Fairbairn shook his head again. "She won't get in there anyway. Japanese troops on one side, Japanese police on the other. Refugees flooding into the International Settlement constantly, the Japanese searching everyone leaving the Chinese district. We're trying to lend a hand while remaining neutral, but it's hard."

"They might try to get the contraband to Nanking. Mrs. Lee is from there so her husband's businesses are there, too."

Fairbairn pursed his thin lips. "Yes. Lee Jinguo died about two years ago, left a young widow. Could be her. I only know the name because he has a file here in Shanghai. Very clever old fellow. Accused of smuggling. Opium mostly. He was never caught but we kept an eye on him. He had a sort of love/hate relationship with our own group of gangsters like Du Yuesheng. Any businesses he had here were legitimate, some factories and shipping. Now his widow is keeping the business going, eh?"

"I don't know how much of the less legitimate side she is still running. Smuggling, certainly. She said she wants to hire an army."

Fairbairn chuckled. "That's a new one. What for, to protect her from other gangsters?"

"I'll let you know when I find out."

Fairbairn opened his hands. The old knife scars were prominent on his tanned skin. "I'd give you any assistance you need, John, you know that, but we are stretched to the limits. Refugees escaping the Chinese sectors. Riots. The fighting. Any minute we expect a bomb to drop on us, either from the Japanese or the Chinese, by accident or on purpose. And through it all, we have our own criminal element going strong. Visitors still pouring in as though we aren't on the verge of all out war."

"I didn't expect anything, William," Falco admitted. "Just wanted to give you the courtesy of letting you know what I'm involved in. I don't want to step on your toes."

"Sorry I can't at least find that junk for you. Not much to go on and I haven't the men."

Falco waved a dismissive hand. "Don't worry about it. Petrov and Mie Lee will know where it's going. I'll get to the bottom of it."

He left the police station with a foreboding that pushed on him like the crush of the homeless around him in the streets of the International Settlement.

"Where did Petrov send the junk?" Falco asked.

He sat in Mie Lee's suite, drinking a cup of hot green tea. She sat next to him, wearing a light blue *qipao* dress. Her posture was straight, but she sat so close that he felt the heat of her body as though it rivaled the teacup in his hands. She sipped her own tea lightly, her eyes darting to him.

She took her time to set the cup on the silver platter on the low table in front of the sofa. Her maid, Hua-ling, had made the tea, poured two cups, and discretely left.

"So," she said with her lips a straight line, "you do not care about me, only about the gold."

Falco eased out a calming breath. "A friend of mine was killed because of that gold. I want the murderer brought to justice and the stolen items returned to the temples where they belong."

"Even if that gold is to help me?" She tilted her head back to glare at him.

He set his cup on the table next to hers. "Mie, you are already rich. Why would you need the gold?"

She didn't reply but looked down at her hands interlaced on her lap.

"Mie, I said that I would help you. I will do whatever I can. Trust me."

When she looked back at him her eyes had lost the hardness and she looked much younger and vulnerable. "I am not so rich, John."

"What do you mean?"

"My husband did not always deal in legitimate businesses. He was involved in things I do not wish to talk about. And there are other men, some within the government, who see that certain aspects of these business dealings did not come to the attention of the authorities. These are powerful men, who control much of what is done. Both gangsters and politicians. Believe me, you do not want to cross them. They allow me to have some say in some of the businesses and to keep up my lifestyle, but the money that my husband had, it is not mine. It is tied to the businesses, to running them, both legal and not, and with paying these men. Even though my husband is dead, they will not allow his businesses to disappear. They allow me to run them as a figurehead, for appearances. Lee Jinguo married me when I was very young. He was already in his fifties. My parents arranged it in order to expunge my father's debt to Lee Jinguo. He wanted the prestige because my mother had been related to the royal family and I was considered very pretty. He showed me off in public. He did not know how smart I was, but I was able to trick him into adding my name to some properties and businesses he owned, like the factory and warehouse here in Shanghai. That is the only way I could guarantee my future. I also saved my own money. I have some money, but I am not rich. These partners of his, they watch over me and have warned me not to involve myself in some of Lee Jinguo's businesses."

"Opium?" he asked.

She nodded. "Among other things. I have had to toughen myself to stand up to these men. In a way they fear me as much as I fear them. We have formed a truce, and sort of alliance. They still need me the way Lee Jinguo needed me, to disguise the businesses."

"How does Petrov fit in?"

"He's a smuggler and thief. My husband had used him before. He is not part of my husband's organization but he has done work for it and some of the triads. He has also done business with some of the northern warlords. One time he visited me, he said that those men who control my companies were cowards. If they came across the armies of any of the warlords, they would run away. I asked him how much would it cost to hire a warlord's army. I made a joke, but he said he had a way. He was stealing small gold artifacts now and then. If he stole a lot of them, he could get enough gold to buy an army. He would only take a quarter for his part. He even contacted some of the warlords to see if anyone was interested. I could not message anyone or my husband's associates would hear of it. Serge has been instrumental in this, but sometimes he takes too many liberties. He did not like my attention to you, but he saw you as a harmless rival. Now I don't think he sees you as harmless."

"Couldn't you just leave Nanking?" he asked. "Go to Europe or America, somewhere these people have no hold."

She smiled at him. "They need me. They hide behind me. Some of these men, two of them, are highly placed officials in the government. What they do, their involvement in illegal businesses, are blamed on me so that they are free and look clean and pure. I have often thought of leaving, but I would have nothing. No money except what little I have been able to secretly save."

"Start over again," he insisted. "You are young. Don't allow things to tie you here."

She scoffed. "And do what? Be a poor Chinese woman in America or England? Do you know how the Europeans and Americans treat the Chinese? Particularly women? In any society, women are looked down upon. I am doubly cursed. A woman *and* Chinese. I would end up being someone's prostitute just to eat. No, best to live under the thumb of these men in Nanking and show them I know how to fight them. You cannot have your precious temple trinkets."

"What about the large Buddha of Monk Shi? I cannot let that be destroyed."

She tapped a long, enameled nail to her lips. "The Buddha of a monk? Is that what I believe it is?"

He nodded to her.

Her eyes widened a little. "I have heard of those. I told you I am not a Buddhist. My father wasn't and Lee Jinguo certainly wasn't. But I have always had a reverence to those who follow the belief, especially the devoted monks. What if you and I form a truce? An alliance. A compromise?"

"What sort of compromise?" Falco asked dubiously.

She gave him a little smile and tilted her head. "Allow me to keep the rest of the gold and I will have the large Buddha returned."

"These aren't yours to bargain with," he pointed out.

"They are mine for now," she said.

"Petrov has them. What if he double-crosses you and keeps everything?"

She shook her head. "He knows that he would be dead. He would not dare to cross me."

The vicious look that flashed over her face faded away and she moved closer to him, their shoulders touching. "John, did you promise to return all of the temple items to each of the temples?"

"I promised to return the Buddha of Monk Shi."

"Exactly! You can take the big Buddha back. These other items, what do those temples need with their little gold statues and cups? The temples and monks can do without them. I still need them to buy an army to protect me. If I give you back the monk's Buddha, you can forgive me the rest."

He furrowed his brow as he thought of the offer. His promise was to the abbot of Lian Shan Shuang Lin Monastery to bring back Monk Shi. And to Governor Clementi to discover who was behind Butler's murder. He was certain Petrov had Butler killed. Returning to Singapore with the gold Buddha, both the life-size one and the one he had turned over to Hill in Hong Kong, would be enough evidence of Petrov's guilt. If he could bring Petrov back as a prisoner, that would end his involvement.

"Can you avoid melting down the artifacts for as long as possible?" he asked Mie.

She shrugged. "I don't know where we could have that done. Certainly not in Shanghai. Maybe in Nanking, but my husband's associates would be watching my every move and would take steps to stop me. That is not an issue right now."

"Okay. Allow me to take the Buddha of Monk Shi back to Singapore and I will not interfere with your plans for now. Once the Buddha is returned, I will help you against these men without you having to buy an army."

She laughed at him. "What could you do against four powerful men? I told you two of them are in the Nanking government."

He gave her a reassuring smile. "I have some influence in the Nanking government. Give me their names and I'll see what can be done."

Falco felt confident that he would soon be able to return the Buddha statue back to Singapore, that he could prevent its destruction and get it away from Petrov. Unfortunately, he still did not know where the junk called *Lotus* had sailed with the temple artifacts. The Russian was keeping that a secret, even from Mie Lee. She told Falco that Petrov had been evasive when asked where the gold was. He would repeat that it was safe, it was being moved around so that it would not be discovered by authorities, and that he would have access to it when needed.

When he left Mie's suite to return to his room, Sister Catherine stuck her head out of her own door.

"So," she said with a grin as she approached when he opened his door. "What were you two up to?"

"We were having tea," he explained.

She slipped into his room before he could close the door.

"For three hours?" she asked, incredulous.

"Yes. And we talked."

"About what? Did you find out where the crates with the gold are?"

"She doesn't know." He didn't mention why Mie wanted the gold. He felt that she had spoken to him in confidence and that it wasn't any of Sister Catherine's business.

"But Petrov knows where it is," she mused, pursing her lips. She glanced at him, her eyes suddenly bright. "I could find out. We'll all have dinner tonight. Mie wants you to take her to one of those jazz clubs. I'll get Serge's confidence. After a few drinks, his tongue will loosen and I can find out what happened to those crates."

"You?"

She gave him an insulted look, hands on her narrow hips. "Hey! I clean up pretty good. And you should see the dress Mie helped me find. Of course I don't have any money and couldn't buy it, but she insisted. She paid for it, the lovely girl. She's so nice. And she really likes you. She kept asking me questions about you. I had to make things up. I hope you don't mind."

"What exactly did you say to her?"

She waved a hand. "Oh, don't worry. Nothing important. You ran away from home, joined a Tibetan monastery, you know. Look, you were up early. Why don't you get some rest. I need to make myself up for this evening. I want Serge to notice me. I haven't done anything like that in years." She looked up at the ceiling and crossed herself. "Forgive me."

She dashed out, leaving him to close the door.

He spent the next few hours in exercise. When finished, he sat in meditation for an hour, then bathed. When the banging knock on his door started, he was dressed in his better brown suit that had been cleaned and pressed by the hotel and was tying his better tie.

Sister Catherine stood at his door, right hand on one hip, wearing a long red dress that clung to her skinny figure, showing what little shape she had and exposing her arms and back. A choker of pearls encircled her thin neck. Her blonde hair was curled. A small bit of make-up seemed expertly applied that it wasn't noticeable but gave her normal pallor some color.

"Mother Superior would have a fit!" she declared. "Ready? How do I look?"

"You look good. Not anything like a nun."

"Good. That's the reaction I was aiming for." She fingered the necklace. "Oh, the pearls aren't real. Mie thought it was a good accent to the dress and I don't have any jewelry. Aside from my rosary, which just doesn't go with this dress."

"No, I don't believe it would."

"Of course," she went on, "I couldn't buy anything myself and I refused to let Mie pay for something expensive, so we settled on these fake pearls. No one would notice they aren't real unless they examine them up close, and I'm not about to let anyone get that close."

They met Mie Lee in the hallway. She was dressed in a similar European gown of light blue which did show off her curves. She carried a light cape of a darker shade over her arm and a small gold purse in her hand. When she saw Sister Catherine, she smiled and nodded, then pursed her lips.

"I'm afraid I neglected to suggest a wrap, Kate. You will get cold later. I will have Hua-ling pick something from my closet. Just a moment."

Mie stepped back into her suite and came out within a minute with another cloak, this one maroon.

"I made reservations here," she said as they headed for the elevator. "The hotel's restaurant is excellent and I miss good Chinese food."

"Won't Serge be joining us?" Sister Catherine asked.

"Yes. I sent a message to his room. He should be waiting for us. I prefer to be fashionably late. Let him have his vodka while he waits for us. It will put him in a better mood."

Taking the elevator to the eighth floor, they entered the Dragon Phoenix restaurant. They were escorted to a table near windows that looked out over the night of Shanghai. Some of the city's lights burned, but also a few distant fires, a reminder of the fighting that raged during the daylight. Among the pillars of red and gold, the carvings in the ceiling looked down upon the diners. Golden dragons and phoenix circled each other, a traditional image of harmony that was mocked by the outside world.

Petrov sat with his back to the windows, watching the room under heavy brows. The nearly empty glass in his hand held something darker than vodka and it seemed that this was not his first drink. He saw Mie and her party being led across the floor and polished off his drink. He glared at Mie and Falco at first, then lost his glumness when he saw Sister Catherine.

He fumbled slowly to his feet.

"Kate! So glad you could join us. We will have a wonderful evening."

Mie helped them order some of the traditional Chinese dishes. Petrov took to the spicier foods while Sister Catherine gave those a wide berth, preferring milder dishes. Falco, of course, stayed away from anything with meat.

The conversation fumbled for a while until Mie began asking Falco about jazz music. He tried to explain the style to her.

"I have been to one or two of Shanghai's clubs with their American music," she admitted. "Very unusual."

Falco sipped some tea, which was not as good as that brewed by Hua-ling, the maid. It was still far superior to anything on board the *Queen of Sumatra*.

"Not all American music is jazz," he explained. "Jazz is just very popular."

"Where is the better of this jazz music?" she asked.

"Many of the clubs are good. I haven't spent a lot of time in Shanghai but I understand that the Lotus House has some good singers and musicians. A friend of mine used to sing there, before she moved to Hong Kong. She sang in a number of the clubs but the Lotus House was one of her favorites."

"Then the Lotus House is the one," Mie said with finality.

Falco wondered if it was still open in these times. It was located in the French Concession, so it should be safe from the fighting.

Petrov polished of yet another glass of liquor and offered a comment. "This American jazz. I do not understand it."

Sister Catherine patted his arm. "Just give it a try, Serge. You might enjoy it."

When dinner was concluded and the plates cleared away, they headed for the elevator to the hotel's lobby. Mie stopped to the concierge to request a taxicab.

The doorman held open the doors for Mie and her guests, and they were soon rolling through the streets of Shanghai. Soldiers at checkpoints stopped the cab several times to examine the driver and passengers, checking their identifications. First were United States Marines. Then British Army. Finally members of the French Army, once they entered the French Concession. They arrived at a building with a neon sign declaring it the Lotus House. Many of the clubs along these streets were dark, closed down. Only a handful were still open for business. French police and soldiers patrolled the quiet streets. There were more military and police vehicles than cabs.

At the doors to the club, two brawny Chinese in European suits stood on either side and scrutinized everyone entering.

Inside the wide, smoky room, the tables were only half full, but the band playing was just as loud as if there was standing room only. The five musicians wore black tuxedos and played instruments including drums, trumpet, trombone, clarinet and piano. Each were young Chinese men, enthusiastically playing *Bye Bye Blackbird.*

Mie Lee's group was seated at a round table to the right of the stage. A waitress in a short version of a tradition Chinese dress came and asked for their drink orders. While Petrov asked for scotch, Mie ordered champagne for her and Kate. Falco shook his head, opting for no drink at all.

When the song was done, Petrov made a face.

"Is not like Russian song." Then he began to drone in Russian and slap the table in rhythm until his drink arrived.

When the band began playing again, a young Chinese girl in a sequin European-style gown came on stage to sing.

Mie leaned close to Falco. "It is rather nice music. I think I like it."

Sister Catherine's face wore a smile, but to Falco it seemed forced. She didn't make any comment. When the champagne was poured, she took sips at first, began giggling, then took some deeper swallows. Falco worried she might take to the alcohol and forget her original plan, but she talked with Petrov and joked with him. The Russian did seem to loosen his mood with her.

Falco decided to settle back and enjoy the music, take later to worry about how he would find the gold Buddha of Monk Shi.

Until he saw a group enter the club.

Three older Chinese men, two in suits and one in a long traditional black silk jacket with a high collar. Each man was accompanied by an overly made-up Chinese girl decades younger than their escorts. Behind the group, two tall Eastern European men followed, their dark eyes glaring at everyone in the room.

The man in the silk Chinese jacket was narrow and had prominent ears, giving him a nickname since his youth. "Big-ears." The biggest crime lord in Shanghai, Du Yuesheng.

They passed among the tables, led by the manager of the Lotus House, to a round table nestled on the far side of the room, close to the stage. The manager, Falco recalling his name as Peng, waved over a waitress to have champagne brought. The pudgy man was smiling nervously, his wide brow glistening with perspiration.

Du Yuesheng seemed pleased with the service and gave a nod of approval. Then he glanced across the room and he locked eyes with Falco. For a moment his eyes narrowed, then his face brightened with a smile and a motion of recognition. When he noticed the woman seated next to Falco, his eyes narrowed again. He raised his hand to gesture to one of his bodyguards, bringing the tall European to his side. The Russian bent down to receive words from Du in his ear. He nodded, then returned to stand in the shadows with his partner.

They did not look at Falco and his companions any more, which did not ease Falco's mind. What had Du Yuesheng told his bodyguard? Why did the sight of Mie Lee disturb the most powerful gangster in Shanghai?

13

Petrov invited Sister Catherine to the bar. That was the last Falco saw of either of them.

Mie leaned close to him during the music, noticing him as he kept looking around for the nun and not finding her. The Lotus House had filled up more over the past hour but it was still not crowded enough to loose sight of people. Even in the low lighting and the haze of cigarette smoke. They had left the club.

Mie placed her hand over his. "Don't worry about Kate. She is a big girl. She can take care of herself. Serge will not take advantage of her. I think he is afraid of you."

"I doubt that. He's a big guy. I don't think he's afraid of anyone."

"Oh, he puts on a front. Big bad Russian. But he noticed someone here who terrifies him even though he has done work for him."

Falco glanced across the room. "Do you mean Du Yuesheng?"

She gave him a brief look of surprise. "You know him?"

"Our paths have crossed a couple of times."

Mie pursed her lips and raised her brows. "I'm impressed. It is as though he doesn't even make you nervous."

Falco shrugged. "Our meetings have been respectful, so far."

She gave a laugh. "You say that as though it would be a small matter if you were enemies. Do you not fear him? Or perhaps you do not understand the type of man he is."

"Oh, I know what type of man he is. I grew up with that type around me." For the sake of the lie Sister Catherine had perpetuated that they were brother and sister, he did not reveal that his own father was a big gangster in New York, head of a large mob. He preferred to steer the conversation in a different direction, but he was curious.

"Mie, was Du an associate of your husband? He seemed to recognize you."

"More like rivals. They did business with each other and my husband worked against him just as often. They were not always on good terms."

He bent close to her so that she could hear him over the musicians who started a new, very loud, song. "What about you?"

She tilted her head sideways. "I have done some business with him. We have met in negotiations a few times. I am the face of my husband's businesses. I have had to come to Shanghai now and then to make arrangements, to appease the local triads, to make compromises. Too many compromises."

She moved closer to him.

"Please, John, can we go somewhere else? Even back to the hotel. Du Yuesheng may not make you nervous, but he does me. I would like to forget about my husband for a while."

He wondered where Sister Catherine had gotten to but, as Mie had put it, she was a big girl. She wasn't his sister and he did not have the responsibility to watch over her. Petrov was a criminal, but she was aware of this. She had likely dealt with dangerous people in her calling. She should know what she had gotten herself into. It wasn't up to him to babysit her. He hadn't even wanted her along in this matter. In fact, he was starting to feel sorry for Petrov.

He got up and pulled Mie's chair back for her. He dropped some bills on the table that would well cover the drinks and took Mie's arm to escort her out. He did not look in the direction of the table across the room but he felt the eyes of Du Yuesheng follow his every move.

Once in the dark street, he could not shake the sensation that he was watched, although he saw no one around that paid him and Mie the slightest notice. There were only a few rickshaws but he felt a taxi would be more appropriate to return them to the International Settlement. They had to wait for a cab to slow down and stop in front of the Lotus House. After a group of Americans sailors had climbed from the back of the cab, he and Mie took their place and Falco told the Chinese driver to take them to the Fairmont.

He returned Mie to her room and looked forward to spending some time in his own room in exercise and meditation when Mie took his hand and asked him to stay. She called to Hua-ling to prepare some tea, and they settled on the sofa. No sooner had they sat than she stood up, arms wrapped around her.

"I must change. I won't be a moment."

It seemed less than a minute before she was back, wearing a thin, silk robe that reached to her bare feet. She sat next to him of the sofa and shivered, though the night was still warm. He put his arm around her and she snuggled into him, her head on his chest.

Hua-ling brought the tea, set the tray on the table in front of them, poured tea into two cups, then left for her own room.

In the silence they sat until the tea got cold.

When Falco left Mie Lee's suite, the sun was peeking through the windows. He intended to retire to his room for some meditation. Unlocking the door, he stopped when he heard the elevator open at the end of the hall. Sister Catherine stumbled out of the car, both red shoes dangling by their straps held in her left hand. Her hair was mussed, no longer the perfect curls. She sang without words some song that Falco found unrecognizable. He watched as she took deliberate steps down the hallway, wavering to the left.

"You look like you enjoyed yourself," Falco said.

She grinned, seeing him at his door.

"It was nice. I haven't been out for ages. It was good to just … be free." She threw her arms out, as though she were flying, dropping one shoe in the process. Her words were slow and only moderately slurred.

He bent over to pick up the fallen pump and she breezed past him into his room. Morning light streamed through the windows. Sister Catherine threw herself onto his sofa.

Falco closed the door. Whatever had transpired between her and the Russian must not have been too terrible. She seemed to be in a good mood from an enjoyable evening on the town. He tossed her shoe onto the sofa next to her.

"Did you learn anything?" he asked, wondering if she would even remember if she had or not.

She nodded her head in exaggerated movements. "Oh yeah. Serge is actually a lot of fun. A bit stuffy at first, but he has a sense of humor. Doesn't like jazz, but can't blame him. He likes scotch and vodka. He loosened up in short order. He's really a very lonely man. All he wanted to do was spend some time with me. We went to a few clubs until we found one with music he liked. Then there was a place where they were playing cards. Don't understand the game, but Serge won some money. Say, the sun's coming out. It's morning."

Her eyes narrowed in on him and she squinted as though to bring him into focus. "You were just coming in yourself. Where have you been all night? With Mie Lee?"

"Never mind. Why don't you go to your own room and get some sleep."

He took her arm and guided her to her feet, handed her shoes to her, and helped her to the door while she protested by shaking her head several times, which seemed to make her dizzy.

When he flung open his door, he found two tall, broad men in dark suits standing in the opening. Falco knew them to be Russians because he immediately recognized them as Du Yuesheng's bodyguards.

"Can I help you?" he asked innocently in Chinese.

"You come," the one said.

He did not appear aggressive but that could quickly change. He felt confident that he could handle the two, as long as they did not have an opportunity to pull out the guns poorly concealed under their jackets.

Falco turned to Sister Catherine. "Go ahead and stay here until you feel better. I won't be long." He hoped.

"*Nyet*," said the second Russian. He looked at his partner and a sort of psychic dialog seemed to play out.

The first one nodded. "Both. Come."

"Okay, Sister Catherine, let's get your shoes back on. We're going for a little visit."

She brightened. "Oh good! I was getting bored. And I'm not a bit tired."

14

At the front of the Fairmont, a town car waited with a Chinese in a chauffeur's uniform. One Russian got in beside the driver while the second held open the back door for Sister Catherine and Falco.

In Falco's mind, he envisioned how he might disarm their escort, disable the man up front, and escape any problems. He felt sorry that he might have to kill one or both, but there might be a chance that Sister Catherine could be hurt if he didn't act quickly and decisively. For the time being, he sat calmly, his muscles tight like an over-wound spring.

They pulled to a large house on Rue Wagner in the French Concession, Number 216. Both bodyguards escorted them through the gate into the courtyard beneath two three story mansions. One Russian led them to the mansion of the right, the second bodyguard trailing them closely. They entered a grand hall and went to a spacious sitting room to the right, where expensive and tasteful furniture sat around beneath classic Chinese paintings.

Falco supported Sister Catherine with a firm hand on her right elbow as he kept her walking steady beside him. The first Russian motioned to a sofa and Falco sat Sister Catherine down. He stood over her, just to the right of the sofa, and eyed the bodyguards. They withdrew from the room and a small, young Chinese girl entered carrying a tray with a tea pot and three glazed cups featuring cherry blossoms.

She set the tray down, filled the cups with steaming jasmine tea, bowed, and withdrew.

Du Yuesheng entered in a long black silk coat. His lined face creased with a smile. He approached Falco and bowed, one hand over fist. Falco returned the bow.

"Please, Master Falco," Du said in Chinese, pronouncing his name as Faw-ko, "sit down. You and the lady are my guests. Please join me in some delicious tea. My apologies for disturbing you at this hour. I thought it best. My wives and children are still asleep."

"I am grateful for the hospitality," Falco said as he took the seat on the sofa next to Sister Catherine, who looked bewildered over the exchange in Chinese.

Du sat in a large chair opposite the sofa and took one of the tea cups with both hands.

Falco took one using two hands and handed it to Sister Catherine, then took one for himself.

Sister Catherine sipped, then sighed. "That is so good. It's clearing my head."

"May I introduce Catherine Murdoch," Falco said.

"I am grateful for our meeting, Catherine Murdoch," Du said with a bow of his head. Falco translated what he had said.

"Tell him the tea is delicious and his home is gorgeous."

Du smiled and nodded when Falco translated her remarks. "You should see this place when we hold large parties. Dignitaries and very important people."

The rest of the conversation was in Chinese.

"No one in Shanghai is more important than Du Yuesheng," Falco said politely, meaning the words.

"You flatter me, Master Falco. But we must make the distasteful transition to the business at hand."

"Business, honorable father? I thought this was a social visit."

Du smiled. "It is. It is a way to show my appreciation for what you have so recently done in Nanking, concerning a mutual acquaintance. You prevented a great tragedy."

"I played a small role."

"You are too humble, my friend. I have heard of your exploits. My ears are big, yes? They hear much. They have heard that you saved the life of my friend Chiang Kai-shek. Even though the rest of the country, and the world, never heard your name mentioned."

"I'm afraid you might have heard exaggerations as to my humble connection."

Du nodded slowly. "That may be, but you have my deepest appreciation. We did not always start out on such friendly term, Master Falco, but I gave the greatest respect to you. You are a Shaolin. You are a white who is Chinese. Few have accomplished this. And so I am concerned. You were in the company of two notorious people last night. You have a reputation but I wondered if this meeting at the Lotus House was one of your adventures or not. You are not one to keep such company randomly. I shall not pry into your affairs, honored Shaolin, but I must make certain you are not in danger from these people. The one was a Russian of low quality who is known for disreputable activities. The other is a woman who is known to be involved in questionable businesses despite her young years and pretty face."

Falco felt unusual gratification that Shanghai's most notable gangster was concerned over his well being.

"Honorable father, the Russian, Serge Petrov, has stolen artifacts from temples in Singapore. I am trying to retrieve them. The woman is in business with Petrov. I am trying to negotiate with her."

Du took a thoughtful sip of his tea. "The woman's husband was a rival of mine, a very disagreeable man named Lee Jinguo, now some years dead. His widow Lee Mie has assumed his businesses, many that run contrary to my concerns. She has been very respectful to me but she has entered into many questionable dealings. Her reputation, shall I say, is very bad."

"With respect, honored father, she is under the thumb of four people who are using her to advance their own agenda. Two are officials in Nanking."

The gangster looked up at his vaulted ceiling for a time. He emptied his tea and set the cup on the tray.

"Do you believe her?" he asked.

"Yes. But I have not had the opportunity to research the situation."

"You are a Shaolin. You seek the best in people. I am more realistic. I would warn you to be careful of her but I will keep your council in mind. I would take the names of her four associates and see what I can learn. We both have acquaintances within the Nanking government. But I suspect this is secondary to your prime objective of returning to the temples that which has been taken."

"Yes," Falco answered.

Du looked at Sister Catherine. She was staring at her tea, appearing oblivious to the conversation in a language she did not understand.

"And this woman?" Du asked Falco. "How is she connected to your mission?"

"She is the one who initially connected the thefts to Serge Petrov. She invited herself along but has proven helpful."

Du pursed his lips in displeasure. "A strong-willed woman. American, correct? You should watch this one, too. If you wish, I may have one of my associates join you in your endeavors."

"Thank you but I do not believe it will be necessary."

"In that case," Du said as he stood up, "I shall have you returned to your hotel where you and the young lady may get rest. She looks as though she has had a rather festive night."

Falco stood up, took Sister Catherine's tea cup and set in next to his on the tray. He guided her to her unsteady feet.

He bowed to Du. "I am grateful for this opportunity to visit with the great Du Yuesheng."

The gangster bowed in return. "It is I who am honored, Master Falco. If there is anything you need assistance with, send me a message here. I will do what I can. I owe you much for what you have done. In the meantime I will see what I can learn of Lee Mie's associates. Please be careful."

Falco thought that was rather ironic coming from a man of Du Yuesheng's reputation.

Falco put Sister Catherine to bed in her own room, used her key to lock the door when he left, then returned at noon to check on her. She was on her sofa, wrapped in a thick robe, her hair damp and spiked, sipping on coffee from room service.

She looked up at him when he entered and tossed her key on the table next to the sofa. She winced at the noise it made.

"Feeling better?" he asked.

"Very funny," she replied in a small, strained voice.

"Did you learn anything from Petrov?" He eased himself into the chair across from her.

"I learned he can drink a lot of liquor. A lot. I thought I could handle it, you know, from my younger days. I guess I was wrong. It's been too long."

"Nothing about the junk called the *Lotus* and his cargo?"

"Nope." She sipped her coffee. "At least not so as I can remember." She looked at him with a questioning rise of her eyebrows over the lip of her steaming mug. "Did we go somewhere last night? I get this vague impression of memories of a big house. It seemed like morning but that can't be right. It must have been a weird dream."

He sat back and crossed one leg over the other. "You stopped by my room after your evening with Petrov. Two gentlemen happened to call before you went to your own room and they insisted you join us. And yes, it was early morning. You were up all night."

She gave him a conspiratorial smile. "So were you, I seem to recall."

"The big house," he said, ignoring her innuendo, "was the mansion of Du Yuesheng."

"The gangster?" She spilled some coffee on her robe.

"He was very gracious. We had tea with him."

Her hands shook a little as she set the mug on the table between them. "He could have had us killed, or roughed up. Gangsters are known for that sort of thing."

Falco shook his head. "Not in his own house."

"What did he want?"

"He wanted to thank me for something I did recently to help a friend of his."

Her eyes brightened. "Really? What was that?"

"Nothing important. He might return the favor by helping me."

"You trust him?" she asked.

"Trust is not the word I would choose. He feels obligated to repay me in some fashion. It's a matter of honor."

A knock sounded at the door and Sister Catherine winced again.

Falco got up and opened the door.

Mie Lee, looking fresh in a blue European style dress, tilted her head at him. "I was wondering where you were. You did not answer your own door. I was going to ask Kate if she knew where you were?"

He closed the door after she stepped in. She approached Sister Catherine and bent close to the woman, studying her drawn features. "You look awful, Kate. Did you have a rough night?"

"It was all right," replied the sister, reaching for her coffee. "What I can remember of it."

"Serge better have behaved himself," Mie warned.

Sister Catherine started to nod, then reached a hand up to keep her head from falling off. "He was a perfect gentleman. I think."

"He does like to drink," Mie declared. "The only problem I've had with him was that he gets noisy. Well, I'm glad you enjoyed the evening, Kate, but I was looking for John. Serge telephoned my room a short time ago."

"What did he want?" Falco asked.

Mie turned to him, her eyes wide and a small smile playing her lips. "He was able to contact one of the buyers. They will meet with us later today. They were able to make it into Shanghai. I want you to be there, at the meeting. It will be in my suite."

Falco furrowed his brow. "Mie, I wish you wouldn't go through with this."

She stepped closer to him, putting her palm on his chest. "I need to. It's the only way I can be free."

"You have other options."

She shook her head. "This is the best one. But I want you with me."

After a moment, he nodded. "Okay."

"Thank you." She smiled and stepped closer, then turned to look at Sister Catherine. "We'll have some dinner in my suite before the meeting. You're welcome to join us, but I'm afraid you shouldn't be at this meeting."

Sister Catherine waved her hand. "That's okay. I may not be able to hold anything down for a while. I'll just stay in bed."

Falco let Mie out, watching her go to her suite, then closed the door, leaving his hand on the nob. "Don't go anywhere, Sister Catherine. Stay in bed and … what are you grinning about?"

Sister Catherine chuckled. "She was going to kiss you. She really likes you but she won't show any affection in front of other people. Her culture is like that. Besides, she has to keep up her tough girl image. But you and her, you know …"

Falco frowned at her. "Just go back to bed. Keep the door locked. Order room service when you feel well enough to have anything. I'll check on you later."

"You aren't denying anything, are you?" she teased. "Don't worry, I will be praying for you."

He rolled his eyes as he closed the door. Before heading for his own room he glanced at the door to the suite across the hall.

"His name is Zhong Shao," Petrov said. "Or Shao Zhong."

He sat in the chair in Mie Lee's suite, his long legs stretched out. Falco and Mie sat on the sofa, a respectable space between them. She wore black silk pants and high-collar jacket, sandals on her small feet. She and Falco had enjoyed a light dinner brought in by room service, tofu and vegetables. No meat. Hua-ling had served, then removed the plates before Petrov arrived. She then brought tea.

"He represents the northern province warlord," the Russian went on. "He speaks English after a fashion, which is why he was sent. I haven't heard from any other warlords. Shanghai is impossible to get to by land. Boat is possible as long as it's small. The Japanese are watching the waterways. Zhong Shao was able to sneak through on a junk from Nanking."

A worried look passed briefly over Mie's face at the mention of Nanking.

"Do you know if he stayed for any amount of time in Nanking?" she asked.

Petrov shrugged. "I don't know. He had to arrange for passage. Who knows how long that took?"

"Is he alone?" Falco asked.

Petrov nodded. "He would travel quicker that way. He is staying in a hotel in the French Concession and sent me message. He will be here …"

The Russian grinned when a banging sounded on the door. He pushed himself up, went to the door, and opened it to greet a man in a Western suit. He was shorter than Petrov by a few inches, in his forties, his black hair thinning, brushed back from his high forehead. He bore a narrow, drooping mustache. His narrow eyes studied first Petrov, then the others with suspicion and his scowl seemed to be a permanent expression.

"I am Zhong Shao," he said in a voice that sounded like gravel being ground together.

Falco and Mie stood up when Petrov led the man into the room and introduced him. Zhong Shao bowed to them.

Mie motioned to the chair Petrov had been in. "Please sit," she offered in Chinese. "Would you like some tea?"

Zhong nodded. Mie poured some into an empty cup and held it out for him with both hands. He accepted it with another nod.

Mie sat back down and straightened her silk jacket. Falco returned to his seat next to her.

Zhong Shao looked at him and spoke in English. "You requested a representative to negotiate? We not given much details."

"No," Falco replied in Chinese. "The lady, Lee Mie, has made the request. I am simply her servant. She will be making negotiations."

Zhong's suspicious eyes widened briefly. "Your Chinese is good," he said in Mandarin. "You have a northern accent."

"I lived in the north for several years," Falco replied without going into details.

Zhong looked to Mie. "Then we can talk," he said in Chinese. "What is it you want?"

Petrov sat in another chair, crossed his legs, and tried to follow the Chinese conversation.

Mie began, "I am the widow of Lee Jinguo. Do you know the name?"

Zhong thought for a moment. "It does sound familiar. I believe we have done some business through him years ago. Business that would be frowned upon by the present government."

His scowl lightened a little.

"I now run my husband's affairs." Her voice was stern and even.

Zhong studied her face for a time, his eyes seeming to look beyond the youthful years and pretty face to someone else hidden beneath. He nodded.

"There are others who would use me as a figurehead," Mie said.

"They were my husband's partners in his businesses that you are more familiar with. They control me, like a puppet. And should these businesses come under the scrutiny of the Nanking government, it is I who would pay. I wish to break away from these people but I lack the power."

"You wish the power of our clan," he stated.

"Yes."

Zhong settled in his seat, took a sip of the steaming tea, then set the cup down. "This would not be inexpensive. What do you wish? To eliminate these partners who threaten you?"

"If possible. At the very least, a show of force to be reckoned with."

"In Nanking?"

"Yes."

Zhong folded his hands together, interlacing the fingers and the first fingers forming a peak that tapped his lips. "Many men. Weapons. How many?"

"I can accommodate twenty men at my home. My husband's place is very old and very large. I am told it once housed an army. I need one again."

"This we can do, for the right price."

"I have gold."

One eyebrow arched over Zhong's right eye. "How much?"

"Enough," Mie said.

"Where? Nanking?"

"Here in Shanghai at the moment."

Zhong shook his head. "Shanghai is not a safe place. Property of our people are being confiscated. Our people are fleeing. Is it in one of the European banks?"

"No. It is not in any financial system. It is in a form that must be melted down. We were to do this at one of my factories, to form ingots, but that factory was bombed by the Japanese. The gold is safe, on a vessel in the river."

"It can be transported north?"

"That is for you to decide, once we have a deal. I trust you can make arrangements to take it west, then north."

"If it is sufficient to compensate us."

"Good. Serge will take you to it. Once you see the amount you will decide what manpower you will offer. I'm certain we can come to an understanding, but I will not be cheated."

"No, I can see that. You will be treated fairly. Shall we make arrangements for the morning?"

Mie looked at Petrov, who was still processing the Chinese dialogue.

"He wants to see the gold in the morning," Mie explained in English.

"Yes," he said impatiently, "I got that. I will take him to it."

"There is one thing we must discuss first, Serge," Mie said. "The life-size Buddha statue is not part of the bargain."

He glared at her. "But that is a huge portion of the treasure. It is as big as a small man."

"I made a promise to John. It must be returned."

Petrov scowled. "*Nyet!* It is part of it. If you want to pay your lover, use your own money."

"Don't be ignorant, Serge! It all belongs to me, except your commission. This piece has a particular religious meaning. It has to be taken back."

"And I suppose Falco will be taking it back." Petrov shot Falco a deadly glare.

"Yes. This is not negotiable. And we will not discuss it further," Mie said firmly.

"Fine!" Serge spat out in a sharp response.

Zhong Shao looked from one to the other. "Is there a problem?"

Mie smiled at him and explained in Chinese. "No. In the morning we will all go to where the gold is hidden and you will evaluate your share. Nine o'clock? Then we will discuss the particulars."

"Has anyone else made an offer?" Zhong asked. The warlord he represented wasn't the only one who was in need of funds.

"You are the first who was able to get around the Japanese," Mie explained. "Therefore, you are the first to be able to negotiate terms."

Zhong stood up and bowed. "Then I shall return in the morning. I am certain we can come to a mutually beneficial agreement, Madam Lee."

Petrov remained in his seat. It was Falco who showed the warlord's envoy to the door.

"John," Mie said after Zhong had left, "I would like you to come with us in the morning."

"Do you think it's necessary?" Falco asked.

She glanced at Petrov, still seated in the chair, his arms folded and his eyes glaring at his feet.

"Yes, I do," she said.

Falco checked on Sister Catherine in the morning. She was wrapped in her bathrobe with the coffee stain on it, her hair sticking up. She yawned at him.

"I'm still not feeling well. I'm going to sleep in, if you don't mind, John."

"That's okay. I will be joining Mie and Petrov on some business. This whole thing might be wrapped up today."

She smiled and stifled a yawn. "Great. Then I can get back into my old habit." She chuckled at her joke and closed the door.

When he knocked at Mie's door, Hua-ling let him in.

Mie was at her table, finishing breakfast, and offered him some orange juice and toast. Within half an hour, Zhong Shao came, let in by the maid.

Since Petrov had yet to make an appearance, they headed down to his room.

After a minute of knocking, he finally opened the door with a muffled groan of Russian as he finished tying his tie.

"Yes, I am ready." He grabbed his hat and banged his door shut.

Petrov led the way, hurrying through the expansive lobby of the Fairmont to the street outside, to tap on the window of a taxicab sitting along the curb. The cab took them down the Bund to the waterfront, where Petrov found a sampan ready to ferry them down the Huangpu River. They drifted among other sampans and junks crowding the waterways, past steamships and military craft from different nations. The Japanese were more prominent.

For half an hour the sampan cut through the muddy water, past a few warehouses with cargo ships unloading and loading crates or bales.

The sampan slowed. One dilapidated warehouse sat to the right, windows broken and grass overgrowing through pavement cracks. It was smaller than the others, deserted and abandoned.

The sampan glided up to the wharf at this ruined warehouse.

Petrov stood, staring around him, his mouth slack.

"Serge," Mie called from her wooden plank seat under the awning. "Why are we here? Don't tell me the crates are stored in there."

Petrov turned to her. "No. You don't understand. The crates are all on the junk. The junk, *Lotus*. It was moored here. It has been moored here for the past two days. It was to move if there was any danger of being discovered. Otherwise, they stayed here. They are not here. Can't you see? It is gone!"

"But you said they were to move if they were in danger," Mie said.

"Yes. They are gone. But no sign of danger. The captain would leave a message, a sign, and we could go to the second place. But no sign. Look!"

He pointed at the wharf.

Falco glanced over the weathered wood of the dock. There were some old wooden buckets lying about, scraps of rotting wood, coils of greasy rope. Maybe these items could be arranged to constitute some form of message, but there was nothing Petrov could interpret.

"What is the meaning of this?" Zhong Shao demanded with impatience.

"Exactly what I'm trying to determine," Mie said with a stare at Petrov. "Where is my cargo, Serge?"

For the first time, Petrov looked nervous. "I do not know. Perhaps they had to leave in a hurry, no time to leave message. We will wait. They will come back."

"And if they don't?" Mie asked. "How can you find them?"

The Russian shrugged. "I cannot."

"When were you here last?" Falco asked.

"Yesterday. All was well. They must have gone to second place. The sampan can take us."

He gave instructions to the two men piloting the boat and they pushed away from the dock. Another half hour, and they approached another dock. Two more junks were tied to it, with a couple of sampans tethered together.

"See?" Petrov declared. "I tell you."

"None of those are the *Lotus*," Falco pointed out.

"What?" Petrov nearly screamed. He squinted at the junks. The

Lotus was not among them.

Mie stood up on the swaying deck and drew up to the Russian. "Serge! Where is my gold?"

Petrov held out his hands. "I do not know."

Zhong Shao shook his head. "If I am wasting my time, my employer will not be pleased. Is there money for our arrangements or not?"

Mie turned to him and tried to smile. "At the moment, it's missing. We will find it, right Serge?"

"Yes! We will. They are hiding elsewhere. We will find."

For three hours they floated up and down the Huangpu River and could not locate the Lotus. The junk was gone and so was the gold, which included the Buddha of Monk Shi.

15

In the taxicab, with Petrov in front next to the Chinese driver, Mie, seated in the back seat in the middle, tried to appease Zhong Shao.

"I assure you, this is only a set-back. We do have what you need for the arrangement. Right, Serge?"

The Russian nodded emphatically. "Yes. We have. The boat has gone for a time but will return. These Japanese, they have everyone frightened. I will find the boat and you will get the cargo."

Zhong Shao's jaw was tight and his eyes were slits. "You have wasted my time. You have made a mockery of our clan. You have made our leader a fool. I will not tolerate this."

Mie opened her palms. "This is not our fault. We have the utmost respect for you and your people. I told you I have enemies who are trying to control me and my businesses. If this is not because of the current environment of Shanghai then it is because of them. They watch me, even if I am not in Nanking. You came from the Northern Territories through Nanking. They may have guessed our intentions."

Zhong turned to glare at her. "Now you are blaming me? This is intolerable! Driver, stop this vehicle at once. I will no longer be insulted."

The cab screeched to a stop. Zhong pushed the door open and climbed out onto the Bund as other cars honked horns and drivers yelled in a variety of languages.

"Do not try to communicate with us. Do not try the other leaders in the north. Word of this fiasco shall spread quickly. I will see to it."

"But we have been nothing but respectful," Mie pleaded.

The door slammed shut.

As the car pulled back into the traffic of the Bund, Falco reached over to place a comforting hand over Mie's. She snatched it away. Her face flushed with rage.

"Serge! This is all your fault!"

Petrov turned in his seat in the front to look at her. "Me? No. I am a victim. We are all victims. The …" He turned to look at the driver. Though he spoke in English and the driver had only spoken Chinese, he thought better of referring to the gold. "The cargo, it is safe. I will find it. The captain was frightened away by the Japanese. Or maybe the British. More likely the Japanese."

The cab pulled to the front of the Fairmont and the Chinese doorman in livery stepped down to open the back door, shewing away a number of homeless refugees clutching what remained of their worldly possessions.

Falco climbed out and held out his hand to help Mie, but she shook her fist at Petrov.

"No! I blame you! You are collaborating with the junk captain. You are hiding the cargo for yourself."

Petrov got out of the cab, his face red. "*Nyet*!"

Mie pushed her way past Falco and launched herself at the Russian, shaking her small fist at the big man.

"You lied to me! You made a fool out of me in front of that man, now you put me in danger. They'll be after me now, all because of you. I hate you! I'll see you dead!"

She slapped at Petrov, striking him across the face.

Even the crowd of refugees paused to stare at the exchange.

Falco encircled his arm around her waist and lifted her from the pavement, swinging her off her feet.

"Calm down, Mie," he spoke softly in her ear. "Let us take this inside."

She kicked her feet. "I'll kill him here! Or there! But I'll kill him."

He carried her through the doors into the hotel as the doorman held them open and stared with wide eyes at her.

She kicked and swore in Chinese as they passed through the lobby, catching the eyes of everyone in the place. He didn't set her down until they were in an elevator. Other guests stopped from entering the car and let them alone with the elevator attendant.

"Fourth floor," Falco said. "And hurry."

When he opened the door to Mie's suite, the door across the hall opened and Sister Catherine poked her head out.

"What happened?"

As Falco tried to usher Mie into her rooms, she started up her rant anew, cursing Petrov and running through the events in Chinese so rapid that even Falco couldn't follow it.

Hua-ling came from the back of the suit with wide eyes. "Is everything all right? What can I get for you?"

Falco guided Mie to the sofa. "How about a nice strong drink," he told the maid. He wasn't certain what Mie was partial to but Hua-ling knew and quickly went to the liquor cart and poured a tall glass.

Mie gulped it down and held out the empty glass to her maid.

Her rapid Chinese continued.

Sister Catherine had shut the door and looked questioning at Falco. "I take it not everything went well."

"No. The junk with the crates of gold has disappeared. Mie thinks Petrov double-crossed her to keep the gold for himself."

Mie pointed a finger into the air. "Yes! That is the word. Double-cross. He double-crossed me."

Hua-ling handed her the glass that she refilled and Mie took several swallows.

Finally a bit calmed, Mie sat quiet, her glass held in both hands.

Falco took the lull to explain the events to Sister Catherine, keeping an eye on Mie in case rehashing the situation might trigger her into another spasm of rage.

Sister Catherine, eyes wide, whispered, "Do you think she's right, that Serge double-crossed her and stole all the gold for himself?"

"He's a thief and a murderer," Falco said evenly. "Of course it's possible, even likely. And it's time I confront him myself. I cannot let him destroy the Buddha of Monk Shi. You stay with Mie, keep her calm. I'll be right back."

"Is that a good idea?"

"At the moment, yes."

When Falco rapped on the door, Petrov opened it and glared at him with bleary eyes. A near empty bottle was in his hand. The rest of the vodka was apparently in him.

"What do you want?" he demanded.

"Some answers," Falco said, pushing his way into the room.

Petrov swallowed the rest of the vodka from the bottle and slammed the door. His features softened as he tried to think.

"Look, Falco. We do not see eye to eye. You and I, we are very different. But you are truthful. Tell me, does Mie think I betrayed her?"

"Yes, she does." Falco did too. He had expected some sort of treachery from Petrov, but toward himself, not Mie. He was not about to let the Russian get away with it.

Petrov dropped into a chair, letting the empty bottle fall onto the floor and roll away. He put his face into his hands and shook his head. "I did not do it, Falco. I know you would not believe me, but I tell truth. Mie is not just a business associate. I see her as a friend. I have so few friends. No one I can trust. Her, I always could. Now, after this, I even see you as a friend. And your sister. She has been nice to me. People are never nice to me."

He looked up at Falco. His eyes were red. "You don't like me, I know. Still, you are like a friend. I can trust you. I am not lying, Falco. I did not steal the gold."

"You already stole it once, from the temples," Falco pointed out.

"*Da*. I am a thief. But Mie and I had a deal. I keep some, she take rest for her plot against those four men … her husband's partners. I would not have stolen so many things from all different temples if she did not need it. Too many thefts would be discovered."

"They were. What about Colonel Eustace Butler who was investigating the thefts for the Straits Settlement?"

"Who?"

"Colonel Eustace Butler. British officer. You had him killed. Four Malay thugs killed him under your orders and you later killed them to silence them."

"Me? No! I do not kill."

Falco looked at him for a time. "What do you mean?"

He waved his hand. "Yes, I have killed. Long ago, I admit. But that was to save myself. Self defense. I do not know this British officer. And I do not use assassins."

Falco's mind raced back to the fight in the shop. Maybe it was a coincidence, Butler's death. He had no proof that those men had been involved in the thefts. He had only made assumptions.

"Are you telling me the truth, Petrov?"

"Yes." He shrugged. "What would lying gain me now?"

Falco sat down in the chair opposite him. "You didn't have anything to do with Butler's murder?"

"No."

"Or the disappearance of the junk?"

"No. It was that treacherous captain. I would not betray someone I worked with. I am a businessman. It would destroy my reputation."

"Okay. Do you think the junk captain was just scared away or do you think he betrayed you."

Petrov shrugged. "I do not know. I told him to watch for the Japanese. They would board a boat to search for weapons. The British and French would search for opium. Any would find the gold and impound it and none of us would get paid. He is a wily captain. I have used him before to smuggle. I thought perhaps he would not betray me but who can say? That is a lot of gold. Even that statue Mie promised to you is worth a fortune, several years of living well."

"That Buddha is a sacred religious relic." Falco tried to control his anger.

"Yes, yes. I was giving it to you, as Mie asked. But that too is gone. It is all gone and now Mie hates me, thinks that I betrayed her."

Falco took a deep breath. "Let's see if we can do something about that."

Petrov's red eyes brightened. "Do you mean this?"

"Let's do our own investigation. We both are at a loss right now. We will go back to the places the junk … the *Lotus* ... was supposed to be and we'll ask people around if they have any clue what happened to it."

"Yes, yes. Is good. We are detectives, you and I, yes? We go now."

Petrov pushed himself to his feet. He stood unsteadily.

Falco stood with him and put his hands on his shoulders to steady him. "Not now. For one thing, it's growing dark. Rest for now. We will go first thing in the morning. Nothing can be accomplished at night."

Petrov nodded and sank back into the chair. "In the morning, you and I. I will sleep, then we work together. Partners, yes?"

"Yes."

Falco patted him on the shoulder and turned toward the door.

He slipped out wondering if he should trust Petrov. The Russian was a thief and smuggler. Was he a murderer? Did he betray Mie? If he had turn against her, why was he still in Shanghai? He was either innocent of these particular crimes or he was a great actor who should be on the stage in London and New York.

Before he returned to his own room, Falco knocked on Mie's door. The maid eased it open and whispered that her mistress was asleep at the moment, that the skinny white woman had helped her to get Mie to bed. Falco figured Sister Catherine had returned to her own room and he didn't want to deal with her at the moment.

He entered his room and took a long shower. Then he began working out. Ten minutes passed while he worked on the movements of the crane before someone knocked on his door. It was a light, rapid knock.

Opening the door, he found a worried Hua-ling. She looked at him, standing covered in perspiration in just a pair of loose pajama trousers, then she turned her head to look at the hallway carpet.

"Forgive the interruption, Master Falco."

"It's all right, Hua-ling. Is anything wrong?"

The door to the room next to his squeaked open and Sister Catherine poked her head out. She looked sleepily at them.

"What's going on. John! For Heaven's sake, put a shirt on. Don't greet a young lady at the door in such a state of undress."

He motioned Hua-ling in, leaving the door open as he stepped over to the couch to grab his robe. He slipped it on as the maid hesitantly came in, followed by Sister Catherine, who was wearing a robe over her flannel nightgown.

"Okay, Hua-ling," he said as he tied the robe at his waist. "What's wrong?"

"My mistress is missing."

"Mie is gone?"

"Yes. She woke up and asked for tea. I was preparing it when I heard her speaking in a low voice. Then all was quiet. When I came into the sitting room, she was gone."

"Did you hear what she was saying?"

"Some. She kept saying that she would make him pay. Do you know what she meant?"

Falco nodded. "I'm afraid I do."

Sister Catherine covered her mouth with her hand. "Oh my goodness! She's gone after Serge."

Falco threw the door open and ran barefoot down the hall. He hit the button for the elevator but wouldn't wait. He dove for the stairwell and pounded down the steps. He heard Sister Catherine and Hua-ling following, slippers and soft-soled shoes tapping on the stairs.

Banging open the stairwell door, he could see that the door to Petrov's room was wide open.

Mie stood just inside, trembling.

Petrov lay on the carpet in front of her, sightless eyes staring at the woman, as though accusing her of his murder. A slender knife protruded from his chest.

16

"Oh my goodness!" cried Sister Catherine.

A door down the hallway opened and an elderly man peeked out. Across from him, a portly man with a thick, drooping mustache stepped into the hall.

"Looks like that Chinese woman killed someone," the second man said.

"Comes from letting Chinese stay here," mumbled the first.

"Anyone call the police?" asked the other, then disappeared back into his room.

Falco cautiously went to Mie. He took her by the shoulders and turned her around. She pushed herself into his arms, her face white, lips pinched, eyes glazed.

"Are you all right?" he asked.

She nodded, trembling in his arms.

"What happened?"

Mie started to speak but only made incoherent sounds. Then she steeled herself and cleared her throat.

"I was angry. Came to confront Serge. I knocked on his door and it went open. It wasn't closed tight. He was laying there, dead. Oh my God, John. They found me. They know I was trying to buy help from the warlords. They killed Serge as a warning. They might kill me next. Or you, to keep me under their control. They know."

"Calm down, Mie," he told her. "Let's get you back to your room."

"Not so fast, mister!" came a British voice behind them.

A middle-aged man in the khaki uniform of a sergeant from the Shanghai Municipal Police stood in the hall, two Chinese in constable uniforms behind him. The sergeant looked past Falco and Mie to the body on the floor. He laid his right hand over his Webley in its white holster and motioned with his left.

"Both of you, now. Come out here."

He motioned to his two Chinese constables. "Handcuffs."

Falco put out his hands. "Wait! This is a friend of ours. We discovered him dead."

The elderly man down the hall wrapped his robe around his pajamas and stepped into the hallway, wagging his finger. "I remember you two from earlier this evening. And that dead man, yes. I remember. That woman was screaming in front of the hotel about killing that man. Obviously she followed through with her threat."

The sergeant glared at Mie. "Is this true? What's your name, miss."

"Mie Lee," Mie said in a small voice.

The sergeant smiled, pleased with himself. "So you killed him, stabbed the poor bloke in the heart. Not a lot of blood. You must have done this sort of thing before, eh?"

"She didn't kill him," Falco insisted.

"Tell that to the inspector. You're both coming to the station."

"I want you to contact William Ewart Fairbairn."

The sergeant looked puzzled. "How do you know him?"

"We've worked together before," Falco explained.

"Well, I'm not waking a man just on your say-so. It's to the station for you both. Chen, use the phone in the room and call the station to have an inspector come over right away. I think Inspector Quigley's on duty. Tell him a Chinese woman killed a white man."

The sergeant motioned to Sister Catherine and Hua-ling. "Who are you two? Guests of the hotel, obviously. What's your involvement?"

Hua-ling bowed and spoke in a low, quiet voice. "I am maid to Madam Lee."

"What about you, miss?" the sergeant demanded of Sister Catherine. "What your name and your business here."

"I am Kate Murdoch. This man is my brother. We were associated with the deceased."

"Oh, so you knew the dead man. Well, both of you will just wait until the inspector gets here. He'll sort you out. In the meantime, I'll take your statements." He reached into the breast pocket of his uniform tunic and removed a small, worn notebook and the stub of a pencil. He flipped open the notebook and licked the tip of his pencil. "Now, what's the name again? And you witnessed the murder?"

"No, we did not," Sister Catherine said. "We all came afterwards."

"Perhaps," Falco said, "your constables could secure the scene, interview the guests ..." He motioned to the people milling about the hallway. "While you take us to our rooms where we can all dress properly. And we could wait there until your inspector arrives rather than invading the station."

The sergeant grinned. "Oh, that would be a fine one. Me and the four of you, and one bonks me on the head, takes my gun, and a murderer and her accomplices escape. And I look the fool, don't I? So just settle yourself, mister, and we'll all wait here. Okay, lady, tell me your story."

Sister Catherine glanced at Falco, then hesitantly began her story about waking up and everyone coming to Petrov's room. She left out most details, went back and forth with events, threw in innocuous dialog that never took place, and included moments that happened days ago, all the while the policeman jotted down notes and nodded.

Presently, a tall man in a tweed suit came out of the elevator and headed directly toward the group. He had steel gray hair, short and wavy, and a trim mustache peppered with white in the mahogany. Wire framed spectacles perched on his long nose. Two Sikh constables in uniforms and black turbans followed behind.

"What's all this, then, sergeant?"

"Caught this woman red handed at the scene of a murder, sir," the sergeant stated triumphantly.

Quigley stepped into Petrov's room, walked around the body of the Russian, looked around without touching anything, then returned to the hallway.

"Just how did you catch her red handed?" he asked dubiously.

"Found her over the body with this fellow, sir."

"With the knife in her hand?" the inspector asked.

"Well, no sir. Of course not. The knife was in the body."

"Then you have two people who discovered a murder victim. Nothing more. What's your name, young man?"

"Falco. John Falco. This is Mie Lee and Catherine Murdoch."

Quigley nodded. "Know the victim?"

"Yes. Serge Petrov."

"Did this woman kill him?" Quigley asked.

"No," Falco answered.

"You say that because you're friends with the woman."

"No. I say that because she didn't kill him. He was dead nearly an hour before we got here. Take a look at the lividity of the body. When we arrived, he was already experiencing *pallor mortis*. It's more pronounced now."

"You know a lot about dead bodies, young man," the inspector said.

"I've assisted the police with certain crimes in the past," Falco said.

"Have you, now? Not in Shanghai, I'll warrant."

"Yes, in Shanghai. Contact William Ewart Fairbairn. We've worked together before."

"How? What cases?"

"I'd prefer you ask Fairbairn. If he doesn't convince you, there is also Graham Hill in Hong Kong. And Harold Fairburn in Singapore. Oh, and also Sir Cecil Clementi."

Quigley's eyes widened. "The governor of the Straits Settlement? Just what sort of person are you, Mr. Falco?"

"A consultant," Falco answered.

"How about telling me what happened, since you seem to know everything?"

"Can we take this interview to our rooms so that the ladies and I can dress more appropriately, and we can discuss this over tea."

Quigley thought for a moment, then nodded. He called the sergeant over and gave him instructions, told him to interview every guest along the hallway, keep the scene closed to everyone, and wait for the coroner. He order one of the Sikh constables to stay behind and help the sergeant and his men, the other Sikh to follow him. Then he motioned for Falco to lead the way.

17

In Mie's suite, Inspector Quigley used the telephone after a lengthy conversation with Falco during which Mie and Sister Catherine, now in dresses, sat quietly and merely nodded when necessary. Falco, wearing a clean suit, was surprised Sister Catherine could stop talking for that length of time. Hua-ling had served tea all around, but little was drunk. Falco told the inspector about the events of the day, explained that the missing junk had a cargo of stolen temple artifacts that he was trying to retrieve, and that Petrov had been making arrangements to sell it. He did not disclose that Zhong Shao was a representative of a northern warlord. He did say that he was searching for this junk in order to return the cargo back to Singapore under the direction of Sir Cecil Clementi, governor of the Straits Settlement.

He could hear the inspector's conversation with Fairbairn. After listening to Falco, dubious as to the veracity of the story, he went to the telephone and had the operator connect him with Fairbairn's home, waking the man. Now he was listening to Fairbairn's words over the wire, his Sikh constable standing like a statue by the door of the suite.

Quigley apologized once more for disturbing Fairbairn at home, then hung up. He walked over to the group seated around the low coffee table and took his seat.

"Mr. Fairbairn vouches for you," he said to Falco. "Told me about you coming to see him concerning this junk, the *Lotus*. Now, let me get this straight. This woman, Mrs. Lee, and that Russian, the dead man, stole this stuff you're looking for in Singapore. Tell me why I shouldn't arrest her for the theft?"

"Petrov stole it," Falco said. "He's dead. Mrs. Lee was his business associate. The most she could be charged with is receiving stolen property, but it isn't in her possession. Besides, it's not within your jurisdiction. The most you could do is hold her for extradition to the Straits Settlement. Not an efficient use of your time."

"And what about the murder?" Quigley demanded.

"Mrs. Lee was either with me or her maid. She did not have an opportunity to kill Petrov."

"If her fingerprints are on that knife …" the inspector began to warn.

Falco smiled and shook his head. "Wouldn't be any proof at all. Petrov was dead before the knife was put into him."

Quigley screwed his face into an expression of disbelief. "And what makes you think that?"

"The amount of blood from the wound. The heart had already stopped pumping when he was stabbed. His body was cold when we arrived at his room. Your coroner will verify that."

Quigley pursed his lips. "You won't mind if I wait on the official report."

"I insist," Falco said. "But you can't arrest Mrs. Lee."

Quigley gave a long sigh as he eased back in the chair. "How did he die, then?"

"Poison."

He jumped forward. "Poison?"

Falco nodded. "No other signs of injury to the body that I noticed. No blood on the carpet. He was poisoned."

The inspector pulled a notebook from his pocket, then fished out his pencil to scribbled down notes.

He stifled a yawn and pushed himself out of the chair. "I'll ask none of you to leave Shanghai for now. Not until I get that coroner's report."

Falco saw the inspector to the door, then turned to Sister Catherine and Mie. The Sister poured warm tea into Falco's cup and handed it to him.

"You look exhausted, John. And Mie, you need to get some rest. It's already morning. We should all get some sleep. Right?"

Falco sipped some of his tea. It was no longer hot, even though Hua-ling had tried to heat it up twice during the inspector's stay.

"I don't think I could sleep," Mie said. "John, I know you deliberately didn't tell the inspector about my connections in Nanking but I'm afraid it was one or more of them who saw to Serge's murder. They'll be after me."

"If Petrov was killed as a warning, they wouldn't hurt you. They need you. They just want to control you, keep you frightened. We'll deal with them."

Mie wrapped her arms around herself. "Without that gold, without Serge, I can't buy the protection I need."

"You won't need that kind of protection," he assured her. "Get some rest. Hua-ling will be here and I'll be right across the hall."

"Me, too," Sister Catherine said.

Mie nodded slowly and went into her bedroom to get into bedclothes.

Falco and Sister Catherine left, Hua-ling locking the door after them. Falco went toward his room. He was beginning to feel the events of a long day. He usually didn't succumb to tiredness but he merely wanted to change and lay down. He vaguely heard Sister Catherine behind him, talking on and on as he unlocked his door.

"This whole thing has just been terrible. I mean, poor Serge. And Mie is so frightened. Do you really think those men from Nanking are behind this? What if they're coming after her? Or you? In order to teach her a lesson, they might want to kill you too. You're sort of her bodyguard, right? They want to keep control of her, keep her frightened. That would do it. Aren't you concerned about those men?"

Sister Catherine followed him into his room and closed the door for him.

"Do you know who was also poisoned?" Falco asked. He slipped off his coat and loosened his tie. His room was very hot. He needed to open his windows.

"Who?" Sister Catherine asked, puzzled.

"The four Mayans in Singapore," he said. He wet his lips. They were tingling. He flexed his hands. His fingers were beginning to feel prickling, like pins and needles.

Sister Catherine looked at him with a sad expression. "I was afraid you might think of that, John."

He frowned at her. His legs were weakening, the tingling spreading. He dropped into his chair. The room spun around him.

"I'm so sorry, John," she said. "I truly like you but I couldn't let you put those clues together. I used arsenic in Singapore but I didn't have any more. I was able to get something from the Japanese quarter here in the International Settlement. Something from a puffer fish. I put some in your tea after Inspector Quigley left. You're too clever. I knew you'd figure it out soon enough. Especially when I leave this morning. I've already made arrangements with the captain of the *Lotus*. He keeps a third of the gold and gives me the rest. Fair exchange when I threatened to go to the authorities."

Falco tried to stand, tried to move. His fingers twitched. That was all he could manage.

Sister Catherine tilted her head and leaned a little closer to him. She pouted. "I really am sorry, John. If I had a brother, I wish it could have been you. I know what you're thinking. Am I really a nun? Of course not. Long story. I'm afraid neither of us has the time for it. It was a way for me to steal trinkets from the different temples until Serge butted in and made a mess of everything. I hired those four Malayans to take care of that colonial official. Butler? They were only supposed to delay his investigation, not kill him. Sorry about that. I'm all packed and ready to leave Shanghai. Be a dear and tell Inspector Quigley I won't be able to stay for the investigation. He'll understand why. Oh, I forgot. You won't be able to tell him anything. Goodbye, John. It's been fun."

He saw her open the door to the hall and leave. The paralysis spread. Soon it would stop his breathing. Panic started to rise. He pushed it away. He would not surrender to it. He calmed himself. Death was inevitable. Everyone faced it. It was his turn now.

18

She felt sad.

She never had remorse over a death she caused. Certainly not with the Russian, Serge Petrov. He got in her way, brought her minor thefts under the scrutiny of the colonial authorities. It served him right to have his gold cache taken and to be poisoned. She had to kill him. He would come after her to get his gold back, and he would be able to because he had the resources among the smugglers. The knife in the chest was an added gift, to complicate the investigation by leading either to Mie Lee or her business associates.

She had no compunctions about killing the four Malayans she had hired to beat up the old colonial investigator, to delay the investigation for a while until she could leave the colony. They had killed him and that had brought more notice to the affair. She had been forced to get rid of the four because they would have led the authorities right to her. Killing a colonial official was frowned upon and made for notoriety. She had learned that before.

But killing Falco … She had no choice. He was too clever. She just … regretted it. He was a good man, and she had met very few of those in her life.

She hurried her preparations to leave. Falco would be discovered soon. The Chinese girl, Mie Lee, had become close to Falco and she would be the one to discover his body. Fitting. So she had to keep Mie Lee busy or she might come after her for revenge. A couple of telegrams sent to her associates in Nanking would do the trick. When she checked out of her room, had her trunk brought down and delivered to the boat, she had the concierge send the telegrams. No way to know how to get in contact with two of those associates, but the two who were part of the Nanking government, Po Chang and Hu Feng, could be reached. She had overheard those names whispered by Mie once. She never heard the other two mentioned, which didn't matter. Two powerful Chinese within the Kuomintang were plenty to keep Mie Lee in check. Too bad, though. Mie had been nice to her, had bought her clothes and treated her kindly.

Maybe she was getting soft. Those years she spent in the prison in New South Wales had changed her, and not for the better. When she was released, she had no intention of going back. Certainly no intention of going straight, either. For a year she had stayed hidden, wearing the habit of a nun, which she had stolen in Melbourne. Nobody suspected a nun and were more often reminded of their own transgressions. It was a perfect disguise. It had fooled the ever observant Falco.

She had slipped away from the others to make arrangements, meeting with the junk's captain, and making the deal that cut the Russian out completely. Serge had inadvertently told her more than he had intended, giving her the place where the junk had waited. The Russian didn't hold his liquor as well as he had thought. Unfortunately, she was a little out of practice and had felt the results of her *tete-a-tete* with Petrov. Prison did that to her. But she had started her plans. She could sneak away and find the junk, begin her negotiations. That Chinese captain was a smuggler and thief too. He fell for the offer and betrayed Serge Petrov without much argument. Sweeten the pot with some cash she had stashed away, then a promise for a third of the gold. That captain could have taken all of the gold, but he wasn't the smartest thief in the underworld. He could have betrayed her, too, but hadn't. He took half of the gold and packed it in other crates, then delivered them. Only two now. More easily handled and disguised from authorities.

By the time she reached the ship docked in the harbor, her trunk was waiting in her cabin. No one had paid her much attention. She thought of herself as fairly attractive but she was too thin. Prison food had done that. And she was still pale. She had to stay out of the sun as much as she could, or she would burn. Little by little, she could acclimate, but the pallor helped in her personae. Once back in the white habit, she was almost invisible. She became a nun again. She liked that people went out of their way to ignore her. A polite nod, then flee from her righteous condemnation. It kept her alone, aloof, and unquestioned.

She checked on her two crates of cargo. Nicely packaged, hidden in the hold, with an innocuous label. Who would suspect?

When the ship sailed, she stood on deck, away from other passengers. She bid Shanghai goodbye. She would have said a prayer for John Falco's soul, if she believed in such things. At least he was gone and wouldn't be chasing her over the China Sea. She had outwitted him. She could outwit anyone. Within a month, that gold would be melted down, sold, and she would be sailing back to Europe in luxury.

Unfortunately, Falco couldn't join her. She would miss him, miss teasing him. She had enjoyed his company. Too bad she had to kill him. Oh, well …

But death did not come right away. No darkness, no void.

He was aware of Mie Lee entering his room, finding him unresponsive yet awake, his eyes open, his breathing shallow. She immediately used his room's telephone to call the hotels operator.

Unable to move, unable to talk or communicate in any way, he sank into a meditative state. His surrounding dropped away. He was not aware of the medics arriving, of them placing him on a gurney and rolling him to an ambulance. Mie was with him. His eyes still open, he saw them take him to the hospital, roll him down the crowded halls. The sounds of many languages came to his ears. Doctors poked and prodded him. He was put into a ward that was filled with other patients. Wounded, sick. Mie was still with him and she put up a fuss. He heard her demand a private room. There weren't any available, she was told. She insisted one be made available.

He was moved from the ward to a quiet private room.

His breathing came more easily. He eventually drifted off.

He let the dreams take him. Nightmares. Visions of gold Buddha statues. Of Catholic nuns in black habits. Of a dead Russian and a pretty Chinese girl. He felt an urgency, with time running out. He ran in different directions at the same time and never got anywhere. Mocking laughter followed him. He was a fool, an idiot. He had been blind and he didn't even know why. He felt the shame of failure. He had to succeed but didn't know how. He was dead. What could he do? It all came to the image of a large gold Buddha who laughed at him. The Buddha was in front of him, taunting him. Then it was behind. Then a mile away. He ran towards it but never reached it. All the while it laughed at him, mocked him.

He awoke once, saw the white of a hospital room, sunlight streaming through curtains over a tall window. Dizziness engulfed him. He let himself slip away again. He felt at ease, flowing in the river of reality, letting the current take him. He could do nothing right now. He allowed himself to float, to be at peace. He pushed away the thoughts that haunted him, the urgency, the failure. He must deal with one thing at a time. For now, he must rest, gain his strength, return to his reality. Sleep.

"It's about time," Mie said when he woke again.

He blinked at her. She was smiling at him, sitting in a metal chair beside his bed. It was a small hospital room, white and sterile. She was the only bit of color, a yellow dress of European design. He remembered she had told him it was French. One of a kind.

He had never felt so weak. Even after a week roaming the Songshan Mountains while training among the Shaolin.

"How ..."

His voice croaked. His throat was parched.

Mie poured water from a pitcher on a stand next to the bed into a glass and held it up to his lips, cradling his head. He didn't have the strength to hold himself up. The water was warm but it felt soothing on his dry throat.

"How long?" she asked, finishing his question. "Two days. The doctor said if you survived the first day you would live. He said you'll need a week or two to recover."

"Sister Catherine ..."

"Who?" Mie looked puzzled.

"Kate," he managed. His throat ached.

"Oh. We don't know where she is. I found you and called for an ambulance. They said you were poisoned but didn't know with what.

At first they thought you had a heart attack or a stroke. I haven't left you. I telephoned Hua-ling to tell Kate that you were here. Hua-ling told me Kate had left. Her luggage was gone. We don't know where she went. I'm afraid I haven't looked for her. I've been here. You see, I told you they would come for you. It's all my fault. I nearly got you killed, John."

He reached out to take her hand. His arm felt like lead.

"Not you. Kate. She killed Serge. Knew I would figure it out."

"Kate? Your own sister?" She looked horrified.

He tried to shake his head but gave up when the pain surged through his temples.

"No sister. A Sister. She pretended to be a nun. Then pretending to be my sister."

"I don't understand," Mie admitted.

Falco's eyes began to sink shut. It was difficult to concentrate, to stay awake. He was so tired. "Kate was the killer," he managed to say. "Not the men in Nanking. You're safe."

"For now. But don't worry about me. I just want you to get better."

She tucked his arm under his blanket and pulled the sheets up. He felt her lips on his forehead and then relaxed to let sleep take him. Before he drifted off, his mind tossed from one thing to another. The Buddha of Monk Shi. All those temple articles. He needed to wire Mzoma and Travis Flanagan in Hong Kong. He could no longer handle this himself. He needed his friends.

Find Sister Catherine.

It became his priority. His obsession. But he was helpless, stuck in a hospital. Two days had passed. How far had she gotten in that time? The junk would not sail far but she may have transferred the gold to another ship. What kind of ship? She had left the morning she had poisoned him. Where was she going?

He had no telephone in this room. He relied on Mie, who was staying with him as much as possible. Even when the sisters declared visiting hours at an end, she refused to obey and those in charge gladly overlooked her transgression in order to keep her appeased. Mie was able to contact Fairbairn and brought him to the hospital, then left them to discuss the situation. Falco was under the impression that her leaving the room was not to give them privacy but her desire not to hear the story again, which tended to raise her anger. She flew into a rage at the mention of Sister Catherine, which reminded her how she had tricked them all.

Fairbairn took the metal chair beside Falco's hospital bed.

"How are you doing?" the inspector asked.

"I'm dead," Falco said, propped up on his pillows.

"Pardon?"

"It's been over two days. I want everyone to believe I'm dead. Spread the word, post it in the papers. Whatever you can think of. I want the world to think I've been poisoned."

"But you were poisoned, weren't you?"

"Yes. Puffer fish. But I had a small amount. Apparently if you survive the first twenty-four hours you recover with no lasting effects. Comforting. But I need to find someone."

"This nun that poisoned you?"

"She's not really a nun, and that's the problem. I've only known her as Sister Catherine Murdoch. She can also go as Kate. Are any of those names real? I don't know. But she stole the gold that Petrov originally stole. She killed Petrov, poisoned him and then I guess she stabbed him to make it look like Mie attacked him or that someone was after Mie. Only making assumptions here. But she left that morning and I need to find her. I need help as to what ships were sailing then. Cargo or passenger. I don't know what name she used."

Fairbairn sat back and crossed his long legs. He pursed his lips in thought, then nodded slowly. "I can make some inquiries. You're still serving officially under the Straits Settlement's governor, right?"

"I guess. I doubt if there is anything in writing but Governor Clementi did request my help."

"Then you are officially attached to the Straits Settlement. You're a colonial official. We can do anything in cooperation of your duty."

"What about my death?"

Fairbairn gave a small smile. "It shall be greatly exaggerated."

Falco laid his head back on his pillows. "Good. If Catherine Murdoch is convinced I'd dead then she will be more brazen. I'm the only one who knew she posed as a nun. The only one who knows she stole some of the temple artifacts herself and that she was responsible for Butler's death, and that she killed the four Malay assassins. It will give her confidence to think I'm dead."

"Right. And the death of a colonial official will go far and wide. In the meantime, we'll see if we can find out how she left Shanghai, if she was able to get away."

"Thank you," Falco said.

Fairbairn stood up. "What about your friends, Mzoma and that Irish terrorist? Are they here in Shanghai?"

"No. But that reminds me, I better contact them so they don't think I'm dead."

Fairbairn turned toward the door. "Just as long as that Irishman stays in Hong Kong. I don't need that sort of trouble in Shanghai. Bad enough with the Japanese fighting the Chinese, I don't want him throwing his bomb-making skills into the mix."

"I'll ask Mie to send them a telegraph."

After Fairbairn left, Falco felt exhausted. He wanted to sleep but he needed Mie to contact his friends in Hong Kong. She returned after the inspector left and he asked her to send telegrams. He began to get groggy and was soon asleep.

He awoke a couple of times. Once was to see Mie reading a newspaper in the chair next to his bed. A second time when it was dark and he could barely see his hospital room. A Sister came in and he froze, his muscles tightening like over-wound springs. Her white habit glowed like a specter. Sister Catherine had returned to finish her job. But no, this nun was short and chubby, older, with a round fleshy face poking through her coif.

She left him with a sensation of uneasiness.

When he awoke to the sunlight streaming through the window, it was to find two visitors in the tiny hospital room.

A large black man stood by the door. He posed with noble bearing in a three piece suit from the finest of London's tailors, gold watch chain and fob hanging from this waistcoat, a diamond stub poking through his silk tie. The second visitor sat in the chair beside the bed, his red hair a wild mess, his suit fashionable if a bit rumpled. He grinned so wide his eyes crinkled, making him look rather like a leprechaun.

"Well, it's about bloody time, isn't it?" came Flanagan's Irish brogue.

"We received Miss Lee's telegram," Mzoma's resonant voice said, "and we chartered an 'aeroplane' from Hong Kong."

"Right you are, boyo," Flanagan said. "We just settled in. Are we in time for breakfast?"

Falco pushed himself up in his bed.

"I didn't want you to come to Shanghai," he scolded, "just be aware of what's going on."

Flanagan waved his hand. "Nonsense! Your two closest friends aren't going to sit in Hong Kong while your dead body waits in Shanghai. We have to come and collect your poor lifeless corpse. You be a good cadaver and tell us all about how you met your untimely end."

"I must return to Nanking."

Mie Lee sat next to Falco. She had been with him so much the past few days, these past weeks, that the news sank into him worse than the poison that had nearly killed him. He looked into her sad eyes. There had been tears in them, but he saw that she had wiped them away and tried to clean herself of any trace of them. She put on her strong expression but she could not get rid of the sadness in her eyes. She clutched a piece of folded paper in her right hand. He reached over and took it from her. She didn't offer resistance.

He unfolded it. A telegram sent from Nanking. No name was given as the sender but it was addressed to her at the Fairmont Hotel.

RETURN HOME STOP NO MORE TRICKS STOP

One of her four associates, or all four in unison. It didn't matter. The threat was obvious.

Falco folded the telegram and wrapped his fist around it. He threw the blankets aside and pushed himself up. He was weak but felt better. His strength would return. A proper diet, exercise, and meditation would bring him back. Four days in this hospital was enough. He allowed others to do his work for him, to track down Kate Murdoch and the Buddha of Monk Shi. He could stay idle no longer. He could not allow Mie to be threatened, forced to do the bidding of four corrupt men.

"What are you doing?" she demanded, standing up when he got

unsteadily to his feet.

"I'm going to Nanking to deal with these men."

"You can't! You almost died."

He gave her a smile, gritting his teeth against the aching muscles and waves of dizziness. "I *am* dead."

She grabbed his arm to steady him. "Don't joke. This isn't funny."

The door to the room opened and Flanagan strode in, followed by Mzoma, who filled the door frame.

"What's this?" the Irishman asked when he saw Falco in his white cotton pajamas standing barefoot next to his bed. "You look a bit spry for a dead man."

Falco winked at Mie. "See? I told you."

She slapped him on the chest, nearly sending him off balance. "It's not funny!"

Flanagan unfurled a newspaper from under his arm. "Ah, but it's official." He handed the paper over to Falco.

Stretching out the paper, Falco glanced over the front page and scanned through the headlines. There were articles on the conflict between the Chinese and the Japanese, but one central story referred to the murder of an agent from the Straits Settlement.

"*Investigator for the Straits Settlement Murdered.*"

The story itself stated that John Falco of Hong Kong, on special assignment from Governor Clementi, was poisoned to death at his hotel in Shanghai. Authorities suspect opium smugglers and rounding up suspects from Shanghai and surrounding areas. The current conflict between the Chinese and Japanese is hindering the investigation.

Falco handed the paper to Mie. "There. You see?"

Flanagan motioned to him standing beside the bed. "Feeling better, I see. What do you intend to do. Attend your own funeral?"

"No funeral. Just a memorial," Falco said, looking for his clothes. "Anything on our fugitive Sister?"

"Yes indeed. Mzoma has been hanging out at the police station. I prefer to keep my distance. I don't think your friend, Fairbairn, likes me very much. But Mzoma has been his constant companion, and he's got some good news. Right, Mzoma?"

The big Zulu nodded. "Mr. Fairbairn has continued his investigations. They have located the junk called *Lotus*. They retrieved some of the gold."

Falco perked up. "The Buddha of Monk Shi?"

Mzoma shook his head. "Sadly, no. I was there when the police interrogated the captain of the vessel. Since he was also caught with opium he was willing to tell them about the gold. He claims that it was only a portion of the cache. A woman made a deal with him. A skinny white woman. He was glad to be rid of it. He claims it was cursed."

"But not so cursed that he couldn't take a third," Flanagan put in.

"Mr. Fairbairn has impounded the gold and sent a telegram to the Straits Settlement," Mzoma continued. "It will be returned to Singapore."

"But they don't have it all," Falco said.

"Not yet," Flanagan said. "But there's more. A steamship left Shanghai the day you were poisoned. *The Empress of China*. No Kate or Catherine Murdoch listed as a passenger, but there are some women traveling alone. No details yet."

"What's the destination?" Falco asked, wondering where Kate would fly to. If she had the rest of the gold artifacts, especially a life-size Buddha, she would head for a place to have it melted down.

"Melbourne," Flanagan said. "With a few stops in between, including Hong Kong, which is first on their list."

"There is no evidence that the woman is on board," Mzoma added. "She may have used some private vessel."

"Sure," Flanagan said with a quick glare at Mzoma. "And we can't look into every craft in Shanghai Bay. This is doable. Check this steamer out and either find the woman or eliminate the possibility. Heading south opens up a lot of possibilities for her to either melt down the gold trinkets or sell them to some disreputable buyer."

Falco eased himself down onto the side of the bed. "We'll check this ship out first. She was in a hurry to get out of Shanghai because of the police investigating Petrov's death. She'd want to be gone as quickly as possible and this ship was the first to leave."

"So we storm this ship with police?" Mzoma asked. "Search the passengers and the cargo?"

Falco shook his head. "And if the gold isn't on the ship, we'd never find it. It would scare her off. We need to be subtle."

Flanagan gave a wry smile. "I can be subtle. You and Mzoma not so much, Johnny me boy. She knows you and our buddy Mzoma here. She'd see both of you coming a mile away. Now me, I haven't had the pleasure. I'll catch up to this boat in Hong Kong, sail with it for a while and see if she or her ill-gotten gains are on board."

Falco looked at Mie. "We have another problem. The associates of Mie's late husband are threatening her. They want her back in Nanking where they can control her."

Flanagan took a deep breath. "Then it's settled, isn't it? You and the lovely lady head to Nanking with Mzoma. Me, I catch up with this steamship. It may not have reached Hong Kong yet. A plane will get me back in a few hours and I'll finagle my way on board, even if I have to throw the captain overboard and take his place."

"I hope it won't come to that," Falco said as he stood up again.

19

The house of Lee was a sprawling building in the *Siheyuan* style near the ancient wall of the old city of Nanking. It dated back to the Ming Dynasty, a single level constructed completely of wood, with intricate carvings from artisans long dead. A central courtyard was surrounded on all sides, with a colorful and fragrant garden and old stone paths worn by thousands of feet over the ages.

Lee Jinguo had purchased it when he rose to heights among the local underworld with the opium trade. He had it restored, held court there, took his teenage bride, and died in the courtyard next to a peach tree. His widow kept only her personal maid Hua-ling, a house keeper who also cooked, and a grounds keeper who helped her with the garden and who also kept up with repairs. Only four lived in a house which could accommodate a dozen. Many rooms were empty of furnishings. Three guest rooms were maintained. Falco and Mzoma were given two of these.

The day after Falco, Mzoma, and Mie had arrived, a message was delivered, written in Chinese, and stating that Mie was to be at the office of Shen Huan at nine the following morning. A young man in a traditional Chinese outfit of black silk jacket and trousers had brought the rice paper message. Hua-ling had met him at the main entrance and bade him to wait. He did not expect the huge Zulu to come into the hall and hand him a reply to take back with him.

Falco had written the reply, also on rice paper, with painted Chinese characters that stated the representative of Madam Lee would receive

Shen Huan at nine the next evening.

Later in the day, the same young man returned with another message, more emphatic, that Lee Mie must appear at Shen Huan's office in the morning, in person.

Falco crafted another reply that stated the same words as his previous message.

Mzoma left the house before nightfall to make arrangements for the next evening. He returned late with an attitude of surprise that everything had been done with such ease. The building Shen Huan used was a more modern warehouse, with storage below and a few offices on a second floor. Despite the man's nefarious underworld connections, security was loose.

The next day, Shen Huan sent another message, chastising Lee Mie for not keeping her appointment. The young man who also delivered this looked very nervous when Mzoma appeared to him with yet another reply. It was worded the same as all the others Falco had crafted.

At nine in the evening, a black Ford sedan pulled to the front of the Lee estate. A man seated next to the driver got out and opened the rear passenger door. Shen Huan got out. He was a small man in his seventies, dressed in a long black silk jacket with matching trousers. Wire spectacles perched on a small nose that looked like it had been broken in his youth. Several scars on his face were lost among the array of wrinkles. He wore a sour expression, as though he were forced to visit a slum rather than a Ming Dynasty mansion. His escort followed him to the main entrance. This squat, muscular man, also in traditional clothes though of a poorer cloth, tapped on the door and took his position behind his master.

Hua-ling greeted them at the door, with several bows.

She led them to a room just to the right.

This had been Lee Jinguo's spacious office, simply furnished with a large elaborately carved oak desk. One corner bookshelf held a few volumes. A set of ledgers were stacked on the bottom shelves. Framed pictures of the late owner and some old watercolors adorned the walls. A single desk lamp was angled at the visitors. They squinted at the man seated behind the desk in the room's only chair. His skin was as dark as the ancient wood paneling, since he was a giant compared to them.

Mzoma stood like a bronze statue with his massive arms fold over his chest.

Falco sat in shadows and spoke in Chinese.

"Shen Huan honors me with his visit."

Shen scoffed. "You dishonor me! Who are you? Don't you realize who I am?"

"Are you someone of importance?" Falco asked, his voice hinting surprise.

"I am Shen Huan," the old man stated with indignation.

"As your notes kept stating," Falco replied. "I simply do not recognize the name nor associate it with any importance."

"Importance! This house would not be standing were it not for me. I was an associate of Lee Jinguo."

"But Lee Jinguo has been dead for two years," Falco said with a puzzled tone. "Were you the one who had murdered him?"

"Of course not!"

"No," Falco said slowly. "You would not do such a thing yourself. You would pay to have it done."

The old man straightened his curved spine and glared at the shadows. "How dare you insult me! Who are you?"

"I am the representative the Lee Mie. It was stated plainly in the message I had to keep writing in reply to those you sent. Were you unable to understand?"

Shen fumed. "I demand to see Lee Mie immediately."

"No."

"No?"

"That is what I said. You seem to have difficulty understanding. Do you wish me to speak Cantonese rather than Mandarin? Would that suit you better?"

The old man spun on his heels and headed for the door. Mzoma was swifter. He appeared in front of the sliding panel before Shen Huan realized he had moved. Shen motioned to his associate to deal with Mzoma.

The younger man stepped toward the towering Zulu, reaching into the pocket of his long jacket. Falco had noticed the weight in it as soon as the two had entered the office. He was certain Mzoma was aware of the man's gun. It hadn't been hidden very well. But a Chinese jacket isn't well designed for concealing a handgun and giving easy access. The younger man reached into his pocket to withdraw the gun, probably to brandish it in order to intimidate. He never was able to get his hand free.

Mzoma's massive fist slammed into the man's face. He dropped unconscious to the decorative rug covering the hard wood floor, his hand still in his pocket.

Mzoma bent down, pulled the man's hand free, then withdrew the handgun, a Webley. He broke open the gun and emptied the cartridges onto the floor, then dropped the weapon onto the man's chest.

"Perhaps you will be a little more reasonable now," Falco said calmly to Shen Huan.

The old man turned to the shadows behind the desk. "Who are you? What do you want?" he demanded with no less arrogance.

"Names are not important. I am the representative of Lee Mie. You and three others threaten her. She has no more desire to be associated with you."

"Then she will be imprisoned," Shen stated triumphantly.

"Really?" Falco asked, incredulous. "You and your associates would like a trial? It would expose your involvement with Lee Jinguo and his businesses. You do know there are records involving all."

"You are bluffing."

"Of course I am. You are the powerful Shen Huan. No one would dare confront you. Am I right?"

The old man's resolve began to quaver.

Falco said, "Shen Huan, your business relied on Lee Jinguo, then he was murdered and you used his widow as a figurehead. You forced her to continue her husbands businesses so that you could reap the benefits and not the liability. Tonight that ends."

"You have no say in this affair."

"I do. You no longer do. In a few minutes, you will no longer be in business."

In the gloom, there came a distant rumble.

"Did you hear that?" Falco asked. "That is the sound of your business coming down. Your warehouse and your offices are now rubble. We had a day to make preparations. You are no longer in business."

Mzoma had fashioned a bomb under directions left by Flanagan. Perhaps not the most efficient bomb the former IRA member might have made, but it worked. Mie had given Falco names of a few people she could trust, and he had enlisted their aid. He did not feel comfortable reaching out to Du Yuesheng, despite the gangster's offer, so he decided to deal with these local people. A few messages sent during the day, then Mzoma's appearance at night. With some help, Mzoma had been able to remove certain documents from one place and put them where they would be discovered. He oversaw one man posing as Shen Huan visiting the offices of a European insurance company.

"Fool! You cannot accuse me of this. Did you blow up my warehouse? I will see you arrested for it."

"You have troubles of your own, Shen Huan. The police already have records of your involvement with Lee Jinguo. They have the insurance papers for the policy for your building which you opened just yesterday before you set the bomb that destroyed your warehouse."

"I made no such policy."

"Someone using your name did. With your signature. And an anonymous tip to the police informed them of your plans for insurance fraud."

"This is a lie," Shen Huan insisted.

"Keep saying that, Shen Huan, and perhaps the police will eventually believe you. I imagine you will have good lawyers defending you. Of course, your reputation will be ruined. I wonder if they will implicate you in the death of Lee Jinguo? That was never solved."

Shen Huan looked around the room like a trapped rat. Mzoma stepped away from the door and returned to his place beside the desk.

The old man slid the door open and dashed out.

Falco eased himself from behind the desk and joined Mzoma as they went to the front of the house. Shen Huan had left the front door ajar as he hurried to the street and his waiting sedan.

Without his bodyguard, the old man was forced to open his door himself. Not until he was settled in the back seat did he seem to realize that he was alone. Falco could hear him calling for his driver. He got out, walked around the car several times, calling the driver's name. Then he climbed behind the wheel himself and tried to start the vehicle. The engine refused to turn over.

With a glance to the ancient mansion, Shen Huan turned and headed down the street on foot.

Mzoma returned to the office, slung the unconscious bodyguard over his shoulder, and carried him to the car, dumping him in the back seat. Then he opened the trunk and pulled out the groggy driver with a swollen jaw. He set the driver behind the wheel. With a few adjustments under the hood, the car would start once the driver returned to his senses.

Now Falco had to deal with the other three.

20

Travis Flanagan sat in a deck chair on the *Empress of China*, reading a newspaper, the *Hongkong Telegraph*. He had picked up the paper before he boarded the steamship, had rushed on before it sailed, able to snatch a stateroom still available for the long trip to Australia.

Out of the corner of his eyes he saw the tall, thin figure in flowing white robes.

Folding down the paper, he grinned up at the person passing in front of his deck chair.

"Why Sister!" he exclaimed. "I didn't realize there was anyone else of the Faith on board. Saints preserve us! An angel among the heathens."

He stood up, folding his paper into one hand and holding his other hand out in greeting. He stood tall and slim all in black with the solitary white coming from the stiff clerical collar.

"Father James O'Leary, at your service, Sister. Off to Australia to a new assignment from the Vatican. St. Augustine Parish in Melbourne. And you, Sister?"

The woman took his tan hand in a pale one of her own and smiled at him warmly. "Sister Mary," she said. "So nice to meet you, Father."

"And would you be heading to Australia yourself, Sister?" he asked.

"Yes. I will be joining a missionary there."

"Then perhaps you'd join me here and tell me all about it."

She looked out at the bright sun reflected off the smooth waves of the China Sea. "Sorry, Father, but I'm not one to stay in the bright sun."

"Ah, well then, let's retire to the dining room for some lunch. It's about that time anyway. But you'd better get used to the sun if you're heading to Australia for missionary work."

"I trust I will acclimate with time," she said with a smile.

"American?" he asked as they walked toward the dining room.

"Yes, Father."

"I know a couple of convents in the States. Which one did you attend?"

"Oh, I'm certain you haven't heard of this one, Father. It is so small. St. Catherine's Convent in upper New York State. We had a Mother Superior who was an absolute tyrant. She would make us scrub the stone floors on hands and knees no matter what the weather. Sometimes it was so cold in the winter that the scrubbing brush would freeze to the stones. That was Sister Benedict. She passed away and Sister Agatha took over. We still had to scrub the floors in the winter but at least Sister Agatha saw to it that we had hot water. And soap. A lot easier to scrub with soap."

They found a table and ordered sandwiches for lunch. Flanagan set his newspaper down beside him.

Sister Mary pointed a long, thin finger toward the paper.

"Such terrible news," she said with a tisk. "The Japanese and the Chinese still fighting around Shanghai. When will they reconcile and find peace?"

Flanagan opened the paper and shook his head. "Not much chance of peace there, I'm afraid. And Shanghai is such a dangerous place anyway. Did you see this article? It has been all through the news. One of your fellow Americans murdered in Shanghai. He was working for the government, and these opium smugglers killed him. Poisoned him, it says."

Sister Mary's pale blue eyes became sorrowful. "Really? Who was this poor man?"

Flanagan glanced at the article. "John Falco, it says. Some sort of investigator for the colonial government. An American, yet. Fancy that."

"And these smugglers murdered him?" asked Sister Mary with a inquisitive raise of her eyebrows.

"Oh, it seems he was investigating some smuggling activity. It's rampant through there. Shanghai is a hotbed for crime, don't you know? The poor yank just poked his nose in where they didn't like it and they did away with him. No clues as to which one, apparently. That is one murder that may never be solved. But so many of them don't get solved in Shanghai. Take my advice, Sister, stay clear of Shanghai. A den of iniquity."

Sister Mary pursed her lips and gave a definitive nod of her head. "Trust me, Father, although it may need our type of intervention more so than most places on Earth, I shall be staying as far away as possible from Shanghai."

They sent four assassins the following night.

Falco had expected more. Mie and Hua-ling had been spirited to the Centre Hotel, registered under false names. The other servants went to stay with relations. Falco and Mzoma had the large house of Lee Jinguo to themselves — and the assassins.

When night fell, he dressed in simple black cotton jacket and loose trousers with soft shoes, clothes he often wore when training under Yon, his old master, at the monk's school in Hong Kong. Falco climbed to the terracotta roof of the house and lay flat, watching the dark street while the big Zulu prowled through the house. He had found an ancient *jian* displayed on the wall of Lee Jinguo's office and took it as a weapon rather than using one of his knives. It was a three foot long iron mace, often called a sword-breaker. Falco had told Mzoma not to kill unless absolutely necessary. Mzoma found it necessary far too easily.

By Falco's reckoning, it was two in the morning when the intruders slunk to the main doors. Each black-garbed man carried a straight sword in a scabbard. They weren't going to attempt making the deaths look accidental. He was certain they were instructed to only intimidate or threaten Mie Lee, but servants were expendable and their murders would send a powerful message.

Falco watched from above while one opened the door with a key. How long ago had Lee Jinguo's associates made keys to the estate for them? He wondered if the late house-master of it.

His muscles ached more than he had expected. He had gone back to his routine of daily exercising, though not as strenuously as before, and had felt his strength beginning to return. The hours he had spent on the cold roof tiles had sucked away that strength and he had grown stiff and sore. He was unable to stretch. The best he could do was to bring himself to a state of mind where he could push away the pain. He had learned that long ago from the Shaolin, a technique he wished he had known when he had received beatings from his mobster father. All he had then was his anger. Now he could meditate, ease himself into a state of mind that took away the pain and the rage.

He crawled silently over the tiles from the front of the house to the courtyard, watching the four as they skulked to different parts of the house. Each man drew his sword, holding the empty scabbard in left hand. Two went into the left wing where the cook and the grounds keeper had rooms. The other two went into the wing to the right where Mie's rooms were, with Hua-ling's room nearby.

Falco barely heard their movements. These men were well trained and he wondered if they all knew martial arts beyond assassination. The sounds of cloth being sliced came to his ears from the left wing. The two had coordinated so well that they both attacked their prey at the same time, cutting into the sleeping bodies of the servants. It would take only a moment for them to realize that those sleeping forms under the sheet were merely more sheets, made up to look like a resting person. No one would be fooled in the light but in the dark, people saw what they expected.

There were sounds of surprise, then thuds. In a moment, all was silent from the left of the house.

Mzoma poked his head out one door and held up his right hand with a thumb pointing up. In his left hand he held the heavy *jian*. Falco couldn't tell in the dark but he thought he saw the normally stoic expression of the Zulu was bearing a smile of satisfaction.

On the right side of the house, similar sounds of ripping cloth could be heard from the room Hua-ling used. Then came some mumbled curses. Electric lights flashed on and items were thrown about out of anger and frustration.

"Search the house!" one of the assassins said in Cantonese.

A door to the courtyard garden slid open and a name was softly called. No one answered. Those other two had been dealt with by Mzoma.

Hopefully he had spared their lives and just laid them unconscious with his mace and tied them up.

Falco slid to the edge of the roof above the garden. His fingers slipped over the shaft of a six foot rattan staff, a *gun*, he had lain there. Gripping it in his right hand, he moved over the edge and dropped to the stone path below. The movement was awkward. His drop was off balance. He stumbled, caught himself, and used the long staff to steady himself. The scrape on the stones alerted the two remaining intruders.

They came with swords drawn, scabbards in their left hands.

Falco swung the staff, warding off their attacks, and spinning the rattan to block the sword blades.

In the darkness, those blades caught the faint shine of the stars. It was the only way Falco could see them coming.

They started to widen their attack, so that one might get behind him. He couldn't let them. He had to keep them together or defeat one immediately.

Holding his breath, he focused on attack, not defense. He spun his staff with blinding speed. The two men moved as if in slow motion. Their swords cut through the night air.

The leader had more skill. Falco decided to concentrate on that man. He would be more difficult to defeat.

Falco blocked the second man's thrust, then swung his staff down to beat aside the other's stab. Then up to hit the man in the face. The man backed away, and Falco twirled the staff to strike the side of the man's head. Spinning the staff the other way, he hit the other side of the attacker's head. He spun in time to ward of the second man's blade.

He losing his composure, feeling the drain on his muscles.

The leader suddenly dropped his sword and scabbard and fell down. Mzoma stood over his inert form with *jian* in hand.

The second intruder paused for a heartbeat. Falco took advantage of his shaken concentration to bat him across the head with the staff. Several strikes dropped him to the stone path.

Mzoma raised his mace to rest it on his shoulder. "You're welcome," he said in a pleasant tone.

Falco leaned on his staff and breathed heavily. "Thank you," he said with sincere emphasis.

"John," Mzoma said, "you do not look well. I believe this was too soon after your illness. You have not yet recovered."

Falco nodded. "We didn't have the luxury."

Mzoma set aside the mace and ripped away one man's sash at his wast. He used it to tie the assassin's arms behind his back. He then proceeded to do the same with the second man.

"Did you leave either of the other two alive?" Falco asked.

Mzoma tied the final knot. "They are both well and resting peacefully, though they will have tremendous headaches when they awaken. They are securely bound hand and foot."

"Let's bring those two out here into the garden and we can have a nice chat when they wake up. I want to find out if it was Shen Huan who sent them or one of the others. We'll have to return the favor."

Mzoma motioned with a nod of his head. "You make these two comfortable. I will bring the others out to join their compatriots. We should be able to revive at least one for an informative conversation."

21

Flanagan was certain Sister Mary was Sister Catherine, or Kate Murdoch. He just had no proof.

There were no photographs to compare, only a description. A tall, thin white woman with short blond hair and blue eyes, in her mid to late thirties. Except for the hair hidden beneath the coif of her habit, she matched the description. Even the outgoing personality that Falco had described. He was convinced this was Kate Murdoch or whatever her real name was. The only question was, where were the stolen gold articles and the Buddha of Monk Shi?

Flanagan was convinced that she would not stay far from them. They had to be in the hold of the steamship. Therefore, he needed to search the hold.

Having sailed on so many ships like this, it was not difficult to locate the cargo hold. He had even spent passage as a stowaway inside these holds before. He had enough foresight to bring along an electric torch. He took a stroll in the middle of the night, found the hold, and slipped inside. He began his search, running the beam of the torch over each crate secured to the bulkheads and deck. At least the crew were more methodical than some he had sailed with. Labels were on the outside of stacks so that the crew who could read could tell which crate belong to what passenger. Fortunately, the hold was small and there was not much cargo. There were items that had been shipped from America and China on there way to Australia, such as furniture, household goods, paintings and books, clothing and tools. Of course, nothing labeled stolen gold trinkets or life-sized Buddha. But also nothing attributed to Sister Mary or her aliases.

Frustrated, he began his search over again. Half way through, the hatch to the hold cycled open.

"Who's there?"

Flanagan walked out among the stacks of crates, the beam of his torch bouncing along the way.

"It's only me, Father O'Leary," he replied cheerily.

The crewman was a brawny man in a white uniform, his hair light brown, his thick cheeks pink. He spoke with a light brogue.

"Oh, sorry Father. But passengers aren't allowed down here."

"That's all right, my son. I was just out for a stroll. Couldn't sleep. Tell me, my son, where are you from?"

"County Kerry, Father. A little town called Dingle."

Flanagan smiled. "Ah, yes. The Dingle Peninsula. I'm from Killarny meself. Can't tell you how many times I've been to Dingle Mart. God bless you, boy. 'Tis good to meet a fellow Irishman so far from home."

"Aye, Father. Heading to Australia."

"That I am, that I am. But at least I can spend some time with a countryman. What be your name, son?"

"Liam Connor, Father. But we can't be staying here and it's the middle of the night."

"So it is. Are you knowing the Sister sailing with us? Sister Mary?"

The man shook his head. "I've seen a nun, but at a distance, Father. Is she part of your parish?"

The sailor stepped aside to allow Flanagan out the hatch first, then he pulled the hatch shut and dogged the clamps.

"No," Flanagan said. "We only just met. But she asked me to check on her cargo for her if I happen to be down this way. Not that anything would happen to it. She's just the cautious type, you see."

Connor looked puzzled. "Cargo? I don't believe there's any cargo down her assigned to the nun, Father."

Flanagan scratched his head. "Now I must be daft. I could have sworn she said it was down in the cargo hold."

"Nothing down here for her, Father."

Flanagan put his arm over the sailor's broad shoulders. "That's all right, me boy. I must have heard wrong. She must have been talking about her steamer trunk. I'll not be hearing the end of this. She'll have a good laugh at old Father O'Leary if she gets wind of it. Can we keep it just between the two of us?"

Connor smiled. "Sure, Father. I'll not be saying a word to anyone."

"Good night, then, Liam me boy. I think now I can get a few hours of sleep."

But he didn't sleep when he returned to his cabin. He tugged off his clerical collar and paced the tiny room, watching the sun through the porthole as it rose over the ocean. The stolen gold wasn't on board. Certainly nothing would be in her trunk in her cabin. Maybe a single small statue, but not the stolen gold and not the Buddha of Monk Shi. Either it was somewhere else and she was planning on rendezvousing with it, or he was completely mistaken and this was not the notorious Sister Catherine/Kate Murdoch, thief and killer.

Falco chose one of the lesser assassins to revive. He figured the leader would have more resolve to resist questioning. Mzoma found a glass pitcher, filled it with water, and threw it into the face of Falco's sparring partner.

The man sputtered and spit and looked up at the white man and black man standing over him. He squirmed, testing his bonds, then lay still and tried his best to look unintimidated.

Falco knelt down, leaning on his staff.

"You don't know who I am, do you?" he asked in Cantonese.

The man shook his head.

"What is your name?" Falco inquired.

The man thought for a moment, then apparently decided it would not make much difference if he told. "Ying."

Falco smiled. "Very good, Ying. Now, who sent you?"

Ying tightened his lips.

"Was it Shen Huan?" Falco asked. "I know he was rather upset last night when he left here. I expected he would retaliate. Was it him?"

"No."

"Was it An Wu?"

Ying glanced at Mzoma, then back at Falco. Then he nodded once.

"Good. Were others involved? Po Chang? Hu Feng?"

Ying squeezed his lips tight.

Falco shrugged. "It's okay. If you don't tell me, one of these others will. I will not dishonor you with torture or even death. You and your companions will be released, eventually."

"Who are you?" Ying asked.

"I protect Mie Lee."

"You are a white man. Why would you champion a Chinese widow?"

Falco's expression grew more serious. "Because I choose to."

"You do not fight like a white man," Ying said after a moment.

"No, I don't," Falco replied.

He stood slowly. "If you do not want to cooperate, that is fine. We will drop you somewhere where you will eventually be found. It might be days, though."

Falco turned away.

"Wait!" Ying called.

Falco paused and looked down at the man.

Ying motioned to one of the unconscious men bound on the stone path near him. It was the leader who Mzoma had brained with his club.

"He was told to deliver a message to the widow of Lee Jinguo. We were to kill her servants as a warning. We were not told to expect a trap."

Falco nodded. "We knew this already. You are not telling me anything I did not know."

"Shen Huan went to An Wu, who gave the order. Shen Huan's place, his warehouse and office, were destroyed. The police have been questioning him. He came to An Wu. I was told about it. I am not privy to the details. They wanted to send this message to the widow Lee. They are very upset over her insolence. She is only a woman. We wondered why the order did not include her death but we would not dare question an elder's command."

"I would send you back to An Wu with a message," Falco began.

Ying violently shook his head. "No! I will not do it. I will be killed. My life is nothing to them. Better to die honorably at your hands than to be dishonored and killed by An Wu's command."

"I will not kill you, Ying," Falco said. "Nor will I dishonor you. If

I set you free, what would you do?"

He looked at his companions on the stones near him. His voice grew lower. "I would disappear. I would go south. Nanking would never see me again."

Falco nodded to Mzoma, who drew his long knife.

Ying shied away, eyes wide. Mzoma bent down and slashed through the cloth binding Ying's ankles. Then he pushed the would-be assassin roughly on his side and cut the strips around his wrists. Ying sat on the ground, messaging his skin.

Falco bowed his head. "I honor your decision, Ying." He fished into his pocket and withdrew some paper money, handing it to the man. "I am your employer now, Ying. Take this money and flee Nanking."

The assassin looked around, saw where the front of the house was, and hurried toward it.

Mzoma sheathed his knife at his back. "Is that wise, John?"

Falco shrugged. "Maybe not. Only time will tell. In the meantime, we can use these others to send a message."

"How? Tack a note to the tunic of one and drop the body at the house of one of these men?"

"Not so drastic. We'll keep them in one of the empty rooms for now. When one of them gains consciousness, we can send them off with a message. Mie and Hua-ling are safe for now at the Centre Hotel."

Falco wrote out a message on rice paper. When one of the assassins woke up, Mzoma cut him loose and Falco gave him the paper to deliver to An Wu. The man looked at the paper and nodded. It was obvious he couldn't read the message, even though it was written in Chinese. He was probably illiterate, like so many poor Chinese.

It was two hours before a reply came shortly before sunrise.

A black sedan pulled up to the front of the house of Lee. Hua-ling's body was tossed out and the automobile screeched away.

Falco had seen the car pull to the front. By the time he reached the street, the car was gone and the girl lay on the walkway, her clothes covered with blood.

He checked her and found her still breathing.

Cradling his arms under her, he lifted her gently. Mzoma waited at the front doors and followed him into the sitting room. He lowered her onto the sofa and looked her over. The small finger of her left hand was missing, still pumping blood onto her clothes, soaking them. Mzoma handed him towels and he wrapped the wound, staunching the flow of blood. Her face was pale from loss of blood. He found no other wounds, but her amputated finger was enough to cause her trauma.

"It is they who have sent the message," Mzoma said.

Falco tried to used a damp towel to clean off the young girl's face. "Yes," he said to Mzoma. "A message for me. They found Mie Lee. Somehow they found her, and poor Hua-ling paid the price for my arrogance. We need to get her to a hospital."

"And they will be waiting for us."

Falco shook his head. "Maybe, but they knew we were here all along. If they wanted us, they could have come here, the way they dropped Hua-ling here."

"Unless they want us away from our home territory," Mzoma pointed out. "To put us at a disadvantage. To give them an upper hand."

"Doesn't matter. Hua-ling needs a doctor."

Mzoma laid a large hand on Falco's shoulder. "And I will take her to one. You stay here and I will take her to the hospital. I will use Madam Lee's automobile."

Falco stood up from the girl's side and nodded. "Okay."

Mzoma went out the back and drove Mie Lee's Packard to the front of the house. Falco lifted Hua-ling up again and carried her out, laying her on the wide back seat of the car with Mzoma's help.

The girl groaned and moved her head. Falco brushed her hair from her face as her dull eyes tried to focus on him.

"Don't worry, Hua-ling," he said in a soothing tone. "Mzoma is taking you to the hospital. You'll be all right."

"Madam Mie," she whispered.

"She'll be all right, too. I'll take care of her. I promise. I'm so sorry I caused this."

She shook her head once slowly. "No. Bad men."

"I'll take care of them and protect Mie."

She smiled faintly and closed her eyes as he shut the door. Mzoma climbed behind the wheel and pulled the big car into the street.

The streets of Nanking were beginning to wake in the early morning light. Falco turned toward the ancient Ming mansion and steeled himself. Rage boiled within him. He pushed it back, but images of the young Chinese maid kept surfacing. His hands shook as he clenched them into fists. He closed his eyes for a moment. He would not become his father.

But Mie Lee was still out there, still their prisoner. He did not need to rush to her hotel room. He had made a mistake, and Hua-ling had paid the price. What would they do to Mie?

He went back into the house, a storm of rage inside him. He tried to keep it in check, but it stayed just beneath the surface. He entered Lee Jinguo's office and used the telephone to call the hotel. The operator could not make the connection. The desk clerk said that she was not in the room. There had been some small chance that Hua-ling had been kidnapped while outside the hotel and that Mie was still there, but that chance was gone. They had Mie.

When he slid open the door to the empty room where the two remaining assassins were bound and gagged, the door flew from its track and splintered. The two prisoners stared at him with wide eyes.

In the hallway were their sheathed weapons. They caught Falco's eyes and he reached down and grabbed one straight sword by the hilt. He let the scabbard fall free and entered the room with naked blade.

"You work for An Wu," he said evenly. "He just delivered a message to me. A young girl, a friend of mine, whose finger has been severed. One of you will take me to An Wu. The other one will die."

They both began talking in voices muffled by the gags. He put the point of the sword to the cloth around the mouth of the man Falco had determined had been the leader for the assault. The blade cut it free.

"No, Master! It was not us! An Wu believed the woman and her servants were here. We came to kill the servants and frighten the woman. That was our mission."

"Then An Wu found where they were hiding and took them," Falco said.

"No. He was waiting for our return."

"Waiting where?"

The man gave him the address, but since Falco knew very little of Nanking it didn't mean anything to him.

"What is your name?" Falco asked.

"Qin."

"Do you know who I am?"

Qin shook his head.

"Good. You will take me to An Wu, Qin."

22

The house of An Wu was not an elaborate affair. It was a modern architecture along European design and may have been built by some European merchant a few decades earlier, before the revolution. It was two stories, block shaped, constructed of stone, and had very little character.

Falco had discarded the sword of the assassin and retrieved his rattan staff. Qin drove him to the house in the old automobile they had used earlier in the night, leaving it a block from Mie Lee's house. The second assassin, still bound and gagged, lay in the back seat. Qin parked in the street in front of the house and led the way to the large front door. It wasn't locked, but a man was waiting inside, in the high-ceiling entrance hall with it's wide staircase.

The sentry had taken Falco to be one of the assassins at first, since his clothes resembled those worn by Qin, and took a moment before he realized Falco was a white man. He started at him with the intentions of overpowering Falco, but Falco surprised him further with swinging his staff into play. It whistled through the air and struck the man first on the left side of his head, then with a deft twist, on the right side. The man dropped to his knees and the staff swung to the back of his head, sending him unconscious to the polished tiles of the floor.

"Where is An Wu?" Falco asked, tapping Qin on the shoulder with his staff.

"There. In the dining room."

Qin pointed to a doorway further down the hall, past the staircase, where the scent of cooked rice and pork wafted through.

He prodded Qin with a jab from his staff at the base of the man's spine and Qin moved toward the door, opening it slowly.

At the end of a long table, an older man sat enjoying his breakfast with a pair of chopsticks. Two men in suits sat on either side, also eating rice and pork. Both stood immediately when Qin enter the dining room. They both hurried toward the intruders the moment they saw Falco and realized he was not Chinese.

Falco struck the nearest one, his staff flying so fast that it blurred.

He caught one of the empty chairs with his foot, pulled it from the table, spun it, and sent it at the second man. Falco's staff hit him several times before he fell in a heap with the fractured chair.

An Wu remained unperturbed.

The old man, in his late seventies with a shriveled face, bald head fringed with wisps of white, was dressed in long robes. He set down his chopsticks and dabbed his small, thin lips with a white cotton napkin. His sunken eyes squinted at Falco.

"You must be the troublemaker," he said in a cracked voice.

He reached into his robes and withdrew a folded piece of rice paper. He unfolded it, cracking it, and flattened it on the table with the painted characters on top.

"You wrote this? You are very good at writing Chinese characters if you wrote it personally but I suspect that you dictated to a Chinese. Did this message intend to threaten me? It is laughable."

Falco lifted his staff. He felt the surge of rage. He wanted to strike that bald head, break it open with one swing of his staff. He knew that the brittle skull would crack like a melon. He could take his revenge and kill this gangster with one swing of his *gun*. He looked at the wrinkled face with its arrogant expression and it infuriated him. But something in those tiny eyes stopped him. Suddenly he didn't see a man who had lived far too many years but a man who was so close to death that he was merely an animated corpse pretending to have a little whisper of life. Falco's anger evaporated. This man had sent assassins to kill and to threaten Mie. He had not acted to kidnap her from her hotel room and hurt Hua-ling. He had not known she was not at her home.

Falco leaned on his staff, keeping a wary eye on Qin who lurked near the door, trying to be invisible.

"You cannot associate me with the attack on the house of the widow of Lee Jinguo," An Wu said.

Falco motioned to Qin with a nod. "This man led me back to you."

An Wu shrugged. "That is not evidence that I was involved."

Falco gave a small smile. "I don't need evidence. I am not the police."

"You have no power, then. Leave my house."

"When you tell me where Lee Mie is."

An Wu's small eyes blinked. "How should I know? Are you not her protector? Are you so incompetent that you lose the one you are protecting?"

Falco stepped forward, his staff spinning to point at the old man.

An Wu smiled with yellow teeth, several missing on the right side. "You would assault an old man?"

"A pathetic old man," Falco said. "One who has no honor."

"Perhaps. But honor does not fill a purse or a belly. It does not extend a life."

"It is important in the Afterlife," Falco said. "Where you will be soon."

"You intend to kill me? An old man?"

"An evil old man who would send others to do his bidding in killing innocent people and threaten a young woman."

"That cannot be proven," An Wu said with an imperious air.

"It doesn't have to be. As I said, I am not the police and you will not live to go to trial."

The old man chuckled. It sounded like scraping stones. "You threaten me with death?"

"Me? No. I do not have to kill you. That will be done on its own."

An Wu's wrinkled brow furrowed deeper. His resolve began to waver. "You are no prophet to know my future, boy."

"Your death is written all over you. It is imminent."

"By your hands, no doubt."

"No. I came here with every intention of doing so, but after one look at you I knew that it was not necessary."

"What would you know of my fate, ignorant white man?"

"I am a Shaolin."

An Wu scoffed. "There are no white Shaolin."

"One," Falco pointed out.

"He is dead," An Wu declared.

"Yes I am. As you soon shall be."

An Wu's narrow eyes squinted even more as he poked his face toward Falco. Then he shook his head and sat back in his chair with a creaking sound that came either from his old bones or the chair.

He waved a dismissing hand. "You begin to bore me, boy. Leave my presence."

"Not until you tell me who has Lee Mie. Po Chang or Hu Feng? Which one? Or both. They are the ones who hold your leash, who you bow down to. You fear them, but which one would take the woman and disfigure her maid?"

"So they have her?" asked An Wu.

Falco gave a mirthless chuckle. "They don't consult you? You are not equal to them. You are beneath them that they don't even let you in on their plans. You are not even worthy of their contemplation."

The old man's jaw worked in a show of anger. "We are partners."

"You are nothing to them. A pathetic old man. Even they see that your time is almost gone. Maybe once you were the great An Wu, a terror in the underworld, but no more. Now they see you as a decrepit joke."

An Wu slammed both fist onto the top of the table. The force made a hollow bang but did not even rattle the breakfast bowls.

Falco turned away and motioned to Qin. "Drive me back, Qin. There is nothing more here. If I were you I'd find a new employer. This one will soon be gone."

Qin slunk out the dining room ahead of Falco.

An Wu shot to his feet. "Do not turn away from me, boy! I am not finished with you. I am An Wu! I have power over life and death. You cannot dismiss me!"

An Wu's ravings echoed through the hall as the man on the hall floor began to stir. Qin opened the front door for Falco and bowed to him as he went out, then he hurried to the automobile to open the passenger door. In the back seat, the other assassin stared with wide eyes. Qin jumped behind the wheel and drove off.

Falco returned to Mie Lee's house, leaving Qin to drive off with his still bound associate. They either returned to An Wu or went in search of other employment. Falco went into the study that had been Lee Jinguo's office. He put on the room's lights, chasing away the shadows he had used before when he had met Shen Huan. From the bookshelf he took the ledgers and stacked them on the desk and began with the latest date, which was only last month, two years after Lee Jinguo was dead. Apparently Mie had kept up with these records.

The names of Po, Hu, Shen, and An were never written down, but there were certain names that did appear each month. Percentages of the intake were attributed to these names, though the percentages were not equal. Taking the majority was Niu Mowang. Falco recalled the name after a time. It was the Bull Demon King from *Journey to the West*, an ancient Chinese book by Wu Cheng'en written in the 16th century. It happened to be written in the Ming Dynasty, which was when the house in which Falco sat had been built. Did living in this ancient mansion give Lee Jinguo inspiration for pseudonyms for his associates? Another names was Heifeng Guai, who was the Black Wind Demon. Zhu Bajie was the pig demon, who epitomized gluttony and womanizing. Sha Wujing was a water spirit who did very little in the novel but accompany Sun Wukong, the Monkey King, and Monk Tang Sanzang on the journey to India. This Sha Wujing had the smallest percentage. There was also an occasional appearance of the name Baigujing. As Falco recalled, that was the White Bone Demon.

Falco paged back through earlier ledgers. At some point, while Lee Jinguo was alive, the hand painting the characters changed. Four of those names appeared throughout the ledgers, taking their percentage, but Baigujing appeared after the writing changed hands, receiving a smaller portion than any. Falco wondered who this fifth person might be.

But the Bull Demon King, Niu Mowang, was a dominant force in this endeavor. He had to represent either Po Chang or Hu Feng, who were bureaucrats within the Nanking government.

When the front door banged it was well into night. Falco had not even noticed it growing dark. Reflexively he reached for the rattan staff he had leaned against the wall behind the desk but set it back when he heard Mzoma call out.

"In hear!" Falco replied.

The big Zulu joined him in the office and sat in front of the desk. It was a large wing-backed chair returned after their visit with Shen Huan. Mzoma dropped into it and stretched out his long legs.

"Hua-ling?" Falco asked.

Mzoma nodded slowly. "Her hand has been stitched. The small finger of the left hand had been severed at the middle joint. She had lost blood but it was not life-threatening. She is very weak and is sleeping. She has been given medication. I did not feel she was in any more danger, though I insisted that someone be provided to watch over her at all times. I took the liberty to pay a visit to the hotel where we had them staying while Hua-ling was being stitched up. Madam Lee is not there. When I returned to the hospital, I telephoned the local police. I explained that Hua-ling was staying with her mistress, who is missing, when she was attacked. An officer paid a visit to the hospital, took my statement, then left. They will not offer any protection."

"But I'm sure you paid the hospital staff to keep an eye on her."

Mzoma gave a small smile, with only the left corner of his mouth, and did not reply.

"Why don't you get some rest?" Falco suggested.

"I am not tired. However, I am hungry. Have you found anything interesting?"

"Perplexing," Falco admitted. "We need to pay Po Chang and Hu Feng a visit."

"Can I eat something first?"

"Of course. I don't know where either of them live."

"Might I suggest the associate of Madam Lee who was able to put us in touch with the forger?" Mzoma said.

Falco nodded. "I think we might convince him to help. From what you said, he took great pleasure in setting up the insurance fraud for Shen Huan."

Mzoma chuckled as he pushed himself up and headed for the kitchen.

Dressed in his better brown suit, Falco found a taxicab to take him to Lin Sen Road. In the Ming Dynasty, it was the home of the Prince of Han. In the Qing Dynasty, it was the office of the viceroy. The Presidential Palace was a sprawling collection of buildings of different architecture from different eras. It was the Palace of the Heavenly King, the Celestial Palace and now the Headquarters of the National Government of the Republic of China. The main gate had recently been rebuilt in a western style, with ionic columns, but two large stone lion dogs guarded on either side. Falco doffed his hat to the nearest lion dog, who remained vigilant and impassive, and walked up to the guard in the uniform of the Army of the Republic.

"I wish to see Hu Feng."

"Do you have an appointment?" the guard asked, checking his clipboard.

"No."

"Your name?"

"John Falco."

At the mention of the name, the guard's head shot up from scanning the papers attached to the clipboard. He shook his head.

"No. He is dead."

Falco reached into his coat and removed his passport. He flipped it open and showed the guard the terrible black and white photograph.

"I assure you, I am not."

The guard stood at attention and bowed his head. "Forgive me, sir. I recognize you from last year."

The captain of the guards came over and asked if there was any problem. He wore a suspicious frown on his face.

The guard turned to him. "This is John Falco, the American. Remember? November, before President Chiang resigned."

The officer squinted at Falco, then the passport the guard was holding open. The captain snatched the passport away and scrutinized it. In a moment he lost his frown and handed the booklet back to Falco.

"We understood that you were dead. It was reported in the newspapers. We were both in the palace that day you saved President Chiang. We discussed the article in the paper about your death when it came out."

The guard nodded in agreement.

"The papers never get anything right," Falco said dismissively. "I'm very much alive. Just a touch of death, but I got over it."

The captain smiled. "What can we do for you, Mr. Falco?"

"I need to see Hu Feng but I don't have an appointment. I have something to return to him."

He slipped his passport into his inside pocket and withdrew a pair of wire spectacles.

Both guards looked at the article.

"Did you find them?" asked the captain.

Falco made an apologetic smile. "In a way. I sort of borrowed them."

The guard hid a smile behind his hand and the captain gave a chuckle. "I will escort you to his office myself and explain matters to his secretary. I am certain we can bend the rules."

The officer took him down the wide stone paths to a long, rectangular building with archways along its facade. The House of Government Affairs had been built in 1925 by the warlord Sun Chuanfang and later housed the offices of such notables as Chiang Kai-shek. The captain of the guards strode down the hall on the first floor to an office with a small woman secretary seated at a desk standing sentry to an inner office. The officer bent down and spoke to the surprised woman, then motioned to Falco with a nod to the door to the inner office. When Falco entered Hu Feng's office, the older man was attempting to read papers with a magnifying glass. He was a narrow man of sixty, with wavy gray hair that had a few strings of black trying valiantly to make a last stand. His pinched face squinted through the glass as he read.

Falco closed the door behind him, leaving the amused captain to appease the secretary.

"Perhaps these will help," he offered Hu Feng holding the glasses out.

Hu Feng set the magnifying glass down and looked at his visitor, with a mild surprise that Falco was not his secretary. He squinted at the spectacles.

"Those are mine!" he snapped.

"Yes," Falco confirmed.

Hu Feng took them from Falco and fit them around his ears. He breathed a sigh. "Where did you find them?"

"On your night stand," Falco admitted.

Hu looked up at him and blinked as though he didn't understand what Falco said. "Pardon?"

Falco took his time sitting down in one of the chairs in front of the desk. "On your night stand. You know, the little table next to your bed. You have a lamp on it, and a book. The glasses were setting on top of the book."

Hu blinked at him. "You were in my house?" His voice rose slightly.

"Well, yes, I was. Lovely place. A bit expensive for your government salary, don't you think?"

"You were in my house after I left?" Hu's voice rose a bit more.

"No. Now how would that have worked? If your glasses were on the night stand when you got up, you would have put them on and worn them to work. Obviously they were gone this morning before you left."

Hu's voice grew faint. "You stole them last night?"

Falco smile and nodded. "You and your wife were sleeping so soundly that I hadn't the heart to wake you."

Hu stood up, his face flushing with anger. "I will have you arrested!"

Falco threw his thumb over his shoulder. "Oh, the captain of the guards is right outside. Call him in and I'll explain to him why I'm really here, Bull Demon King."

As quickly as it had burned red, his face lost all color and he dropped into his chair. "What did you say?"

"You *are* the Bull Demon King, aren't you? I haven't figured the others out yet, but you seem the type. And you appear to spend a lot more than you make. Does your wife have expensive tastes or does your mistress?"

Hu swallowed. "Are you blackmailing me?"

"Now would a blackmailer sneak into someone's house in the middle of the night? Of course not. I came to kill you."

"Kill?" His voice became a whisper.

"But you were sleeping so peacefully I decided not to. Besides, I wanted to talk first."

"About what?"

"Lee Mie, Lee Junguo's widow."

"What about her?"

Falco leaned close, his face becoming very serious. "Where is she?"

Hu Feng's eyes widened. "Is she not at her home, the House of Lee Jinguo? How would I know where she is? She had been traveling, to

Singapore I believe. Surely she has returned by now."

Falco sat back and nodded. "I suspected you didn't know. I searched your house and couldn't find any trace of her. You don't have bodyguards or security, so you aren't expecting any trouble. You're just a corrupt bureaucrat. But you are the Bull Demon King. You take the biggest cut for your part in seeing that smuggled opium makes it through channels."

"You work for Lee Mie? She hired you as an assassin?"

"No, she hired me to protect her. But you want to know who wants you dead, right?

"Who?" Hu asked hesitantly.

"Po Chang."

"Po hired you to kill me?" Hu asked.

"He wants you dead," Falco said without actually answering the question. "He believes that if you were out of the picture he can take a larger percentage of Lee Mie's profits. He isn't as influential as you are, but he still has some sway with the government. And now that An Wu is gone ..."

"An Wu? What has happened to him?"

"Didn't you read the paper this morning?" Falco asked. Then he snapped his fingers. "Oh, I forgot. You didn't have your glasses so you wouldn't have been able to. It seems that An Wu has passed away. Heart attack. Something must have upset him."

"Who are you? What business is this of yours?" Hu asked.

"I am John Falco."

Hu shook his head. "He's dead."

"I am a Shaolin. For centuries we have been shrouded in mysteries. It is said that we can walk like ghosts, vanish into thin air, and come back from the dead. You, however, can't."

"You intend to kill me? Here?"

"Me? No. Let Po Chang do his own dirty work. You aren't worth my trouble."

Falco got up and left the office, letting the door close behind him. In the outer office, the captain of the guards waited. He followed Falco into the hallway.

"Now," Falco said, "could you direct me to the office of Po Chang?"

23

Po Chang was Zhu Bajie, the pig demon. That was obvious the moment Falco saw him when he entered the bureaucrat's office. The heavy-set man was behind the desk, surrounded by piles of paper documents and forms. He pulled one from a pile on his right, scanned through it with very small eyes, and placed it on a pile to his left. His office was small, with no windows and no outer office.

He was fat, with thick jowls that jiggled with each movement, and several chins that made a neck invisible. His hair was thinning on top and a bit long on the sides. His nose was short and reminded Falco of a snout. He guessed the man's age to be at least sixty and he could smell alcohol despite the early hour of the morning. His skin had a grayish tint of one who over overindulges. To compound his unhealthy appearance, he was homely to the extreme.

"What do you want?" he snapped without looking up from his work.

"A talk," Falco said.

"I haven't the time." He set another paper on the pile to his left and looked up at Falco, seeing him for the first time. "You aren't Chinese."

"Really?" Falco asked, surprised.

Po paused before pulling a sheet from the right. "No, you aren't. British? American? What do you want? We don't deal with foreigners in this office."

"Exports?" Falco inquired as he took a metal chair from against the wall near the door, moved it in front of the desk, and sat down.

"Yes. No imports. What is your business?"

"My business is inquiries."

"Eh?" Po said with a puzzled expression twisting his mouth.

"I ask questions. I solve problems."

"What does that have to do with me?"

"Do you know where Lee Mie is?" Falco asked slowly.

Po took a moment to answer, and in that moment his fat ugly face went through a range of expressions from surprise to apprehension to fear.

"Who?" Po said, knitting his brows.

"I just came from Hu Feng's office," Falco said. "He was very cooperative. He told me all about you and your arrangements with Lee Jinguo."

Po swallowed hard. "Who?" His voice made a little squeak.

"Lee Jinguo. He's been dead for two years. You were one of his business associates and now you are associated with his widow, Lee Mie. You get paid from her to help in the transportation of contraband."

Po tried to look indignant as he glared at Falco. "Are you suggesting that I am corrupt?"

"Very," Falco answered.

Po pushed his bulk to his feet. He wasn't very tall, shorter than Falco. "I suggest you get out of my office before I call security."

Falco crossed his legs and shrugged. "You won't have to yell very loud. The captain of the guards from the main gates is right outside your office. He was kind enough to escort me here. I believe he is waiting to escort you out."

"Me? I haven't done anything wrong."

"Not according to Hu Feng," Falco said.

Po dropped back into his chair. His momentary bluster and indignation evaporated. "What did Hu Feng tell you?"

"According to him, you are a very corrupt person, taking bribes."

Po scoffed. "He should talk. He easily takes three times what I could. If you doubt me, look at where he lives compared to where I live."

"Oh, I have," Falco admitted. "His home is far more exquisite than yours. His wife has very expensive tastes. You live alone. And forgive me, but your apartment is a pig's sty."

"I am very busy. I don't always have time for cleaning up. Wait, how would you know this?" Po's tiny eyes widened in shock.

"No wonder you live alone. You snore terribly."

Po's jaw dropped open. "You … you were in my apartment? While I was sleeping?"

Falco shrugged apologetically.

"Why?" Po asked.

"Did you know Hu Feng wants you dead, that he is willing to pay to have you killed?"

Po's gray skin grew paler. "You were there to kill me?"

"I didn't though I had every opportunity. Give me a little credit for that. I didn't have the heart. You looked so peaceful and innocent, sleeping like that. Noisy, though, snoring with your mouth open. Did you know you drool in your sleep?"

Po rose slowly to his feet and walked back and forth behind his desk. "You say Hu Feng hired you to kill me?"

"No."

"He didn't?"

"No, I mean that I didn't say he hired me. But you are welcome to make any assumption you want. Just be aware that Hu Feng wants you dead. He is not your friend."

Po scowled as he paced. "He never was. He always said I drink too much, eat too much. He would never associate with me, never invite me to any of his parties. I'm not good enough to enter his home."

"Did you know that An Wu is dead?" Falco asked.

"That gangster? The newspapers say he died of a heart attack."

"And Shen Huan is under government investigation."

"I have nothing to do with them. They are criminals, opium dealers, smugglers. What would I have to do with them?"

"You and Hu Feng were involved with them with Lee Jinguo. Did he kill Lee Jinguo?" Falco asked.

"Hum? Lee Jinguo was murdered?"

"Perhaps. Do you think Hu Feng did it? Some think it was Shen Huan. You didn't have anything to do with his death, did you?"

"In Buddha's name, no!" Po erupted indignantly. "Why would I? He was paying me to … well, never mind about that."

"But once Lee Jinguo was dead, his widow took over. She was easier to control than Lee Jinguo, wasn't she?"

"True," Po admitted, "but I didn't know she would take over. When he died, I thought his businesses would be dissolved and I'd never get any more from him. Hu Feng made the arrangements with the widow."

"Do you know where she is?" Falco asked, watching Po carefully.

"No," the man answered quickly.

"Ah, but now you're lying. You do know where she is. If you didn't know, you would have assumed she was in her home, the House of Lee Jinguo. Instead you claim you don't know."

Po flushed with anger. "Who are you anyway! You come in here, making accusations. You have no authority here. This isn't Shanghai or Hong Kong. This is the Republic of China. Who do you think you are?"

"I'm John Falco."

Po squinted at him. "The white Shaolin? No you aren't. He's dead."

"Can a Shaolin truly die?" Falco asked.

Po opened his mouth to speak, exposing some of his crooked teeth. His fat face drained of color again.

"You are *Faw-ko*?" he asked in a whisper.

Falco nodded.

He climbed to his feet. "So you see, I do have authority wherever I go, whatever I do, whatever government I choose to work for. Where is Lee Mie?"

Po thought for a moment. "If she is not at her home, there is another place. A house owned by Lee Jinguo. We would sometimes meet there, outside Nanking. Maybe she is there."

"There is another person who was involved in Lee Jinguo's businesses," Falco explained. "Do you know who that person is?"

"Another?"

"Lee used code names in his ledgers for you and the others, characters from *Journey to the West*. Hu Feng was the Bull Demon King. There is one who is referred to as Baigujing, the White Bone Spirit. Do you know who that is?"

"No. Characters from *Journey to the West*? Who was used for me?"

"Zhu Bajie," Falco answered. "Pigsy."

"Oh," Po said thoughtfully.

***

Mzoma drove Falco past the ancient stone walls of Nanking to Zijin Shan, the Purple Mountain. The stone house nestled among the trees at the foot of the mountain was small when compared to Lee Jinguo's Ming estate in the city. It had three stories, built with firm stone blocks, and looked like a modern fortress.

After Mzoma parked, Falco climbed the stone steps to the front door. He knocked on the heavy green wood.

Mzoma came up behind him, his eyes narrow. "Is this wise? Going to the front door?"

Falco shrugged but didn't reply as he knocked again.

"It looks deserted. No one has been here for years," Mzoma added.

Falco pointed to the ground near their vehicle. "Tire tracks in the dirt. I smell rice and meat in the air, recently cooked. Someone has been here recently. This forth person, if they kidnapped Mie, may have brought her here because they knew this place was deserted. It's the only lead we could squeeze out of those men."

Mzoma looked around at the thick trees surrounding the property. "Very secluded."

Falco bent down and examined the old lock. He hadn't much practice on one these models, but he pulled the leather pouch with pick tools from his back pocket He chose two to twist into the keyhole. The picks had come in handy in entering Hu Feng's house and Po Chang's apartment the previous night. This was a little easier since it was a bright afternoon.

When the front door finally eased open, Mzoma pulled out his long knife from the sheath under his coat. It was a congruent scene, a Zulu dressed immaculately in a three-piece British-made suit and carrying a curved bone-handled blade.

Inside the entrance hall, dust motes floated in the air caught in the beams of sunlight streaming through the breaks in the heavy curtains on the windows.

Mzoma used his knife to point at the tiled floor. "Many footprints in the dust."

Falco nodded, scrutinizing the scatter of marks in the thin layer of dust, then cocked his head, listening.

Very faintly he heard the rustle of movement. Someone was in the house, somewhere upstairs.

He put his finger to his lips, then pointed up the staircase.

Mzoma nodded.

They carefully crept up the carpeted steps.

He couldn't locate the sounds again but now could smell the telltale odor of food. The rice and pork that he had smelled earlier. It led to a door at the end of the hallway, the room of which would be overlooking the back of the house. Falco put his ear against the door but could not hear anything.

"Mie!" he called softly.

"John?" came the woman's surprised voice. "John! Is that you? Please, let me out. The door's locked."

He saw no key in the lock. He tried the knob but decided not bothering with the picks but merely kicked it. The jam splintered and the door flew open.

Mie gave a cry of happiness and threw herself into Falco's arms.

"Oh John! I knew you'd find me. They took Hua-ling and me from the hotel, threatened us, forced us out here. They used Hua-ling so that I would behave. They cut one of her fingers off while I watched. It was horrible."

Falco wrapped his arms around her and held her. "Who took you?"

"I don't know. Four men, all Chinese. Thugs. They pushed us around. They hurt Hua-ling. Then locked me in here. Only brought food once a day. The windows are nailed shut."

Falco released her and looked around the room. It was a small bedroom with two windows looking out at the woods at the back of the house. The windows were held shut by large nails hammered into the base. A small lavatory opened to the left with a toilet and sink. The only furnishings was a small bed with covers and a round table with the remnants of food in two bowls. Rice and pork in a sauce.

He gently took Mie's arm. "Let's get you out of here."

They hurried to the car in front of the house. Falco climbed in the back seat with Mie while Mzoma sat behind the wheel and drove off.

"Who took you?" Falco asked.

"I don't know. You were meeting with Shen Huan, but I don't think it was him. It could have been Hu Feng but I only saw those four thugs."

"I looked through some of your husband's records," Falco said. "There was a fifth person mentioned, receiving bribe money. Who was it?"

She shook her head. "I only know the four men, the ones I told you."

"You don't know someone under the name of Baigujing?"

"No. Isn't that the White Bone Demon from *Journey to the West*?"

Falco nodded. "Yes. That's the one I can't figure out. The others I know."

"Like Hu Feng as The Bull Demon King? Yes, I met them but not a fifth. I never knew who Baigujing really was. Do you think he kidnapped Hua-ling and me? What about Hua-ling? Is she okay?"

"She's in the hospital. She'll be fine," Falco assured her.

"What about Hu Feng and the others?" she asked.

"They won't be bothering you any more. We just have to deal with Baigujing," Falco said.

Mie Lee took a hot bath while Falco made an attempt to cook some eggs. Over-easy became scrambled. Mzoma went to the hospital to secure Hua-ling's release. By the time Mzoma returned, escorting a weak, nervous Hua-ling, Mie was done with her bath and came into the living room in a silk robe. She saw Hua-ling and rushed to her, throwing her arms around the girl. She murmured comforting words in Chinese.

Mzoma handed Falco a newspaper.

"Hu Feng has been arrested."

Falco unfurled the paper and found the article. He frowned as he read. "Po Chang is dead."

"What?" Mie asked in shock. She dropped onto the sofa next to Hua-ling.

Falco handed her the paper. "That will take care of the four of them. I'm afraid I turned Hu and Po against each other. I didn't expect Hu to become murderous though I figured there was that possibility. I just wanted them at odds, to expose one another to the authorities. I spoke to some people I know within the government. They were going to start an investigation. Now it will include murder."

"And An Wu is dead, too?"

"Heart attack," Falco said with a nod.

"What about Shen Huan?" Mie asked.

"He is the center of his own investigation which started with insurance fraud."

Mie smiled and put her arm around Hua-ling. "Then it is over."

Hua-ling looked at the carpeted floor, her hands on her lap, her good hand covering the bandaged one with the mutilated finger. She was still very pale and frightened.

"There's still Baigujing," Falco pointed out.

Mie stood up and interlaced her fingers. "But I don't know who that is. How can they feel threatened by me? Are you so certain Baigujing was responsible for kidnapping us? None of those thugs spoke to us except to give us orders. They were obviously sent by someone. Are you sure it wasn't Shen Huan or one of the others? Hu Feng would do something like that."

"No," Falco said emphatically. "It wasn't one of the four."

"But how did you find me if it wasn't one of them?"

"Po told me where you were."

"Then it was him!" Mie declared. "And now he's dead. Good."

"No. He only knew where you might be."

Falco held up a finger and went into the office. He picked up the stack of ledgers from the desk and returned to the living room. He set the books on a coffee table, pulled one of the ledgers off the stack and opened it.

"This is an earlier volume," he said. "There are rows of legitimate expenditures for the legal businesses. Suppliers and employees, along with the names like Niu Mowang. Four mythical names that don't belong."

Mie took the ledger from Falco and looked at it. "Yes. I remember the names. He never told me exactly who they were, but I knew of his association with Hu Feng and the others so I figured out who those names represented. When I took over the businesses after his death, they insisted the opium smuggling continue under my direction and that they keep their cut of it. They even controlled most of the legitimate businesses, like the tea and silk exports. I owned them in name, but they controlled them. Shen Huan was the most threatening, but Hu Feng was also very emphatic. He threatened me with imprisonment.

Shen only threatened to kill me."

"And at no time did you interact with the fifth person," Falco said.

Mie shook her head. "Whoever Baigujing is did not threaten me in any way, so one of those four were responsible, sending me this message by hurting Hua-ling."

Falco lifted another ledger off the table, and paged through it. "When did you start working on your husband's records?"

"About two years ago, when he died."

Falco shook his head. He held out the opened book. "Three years ago. That's when the handwriting changes, before he died. I can tell by the painted characters. They switch to a more feminine hand, with a softer brush stroke that had more flare. He was still alive then."

Mie nodded. "He was a hard man to live with. I thought if I helped him in his business he might appreciate me more. After all, I did have some education."

He continued to page through the ledger. "I'm curious."

Falco set the ledger aside and took another. "This one is from the year Lee Jinguo died. He died in the summer. It was in the beginning of the year that Baigujing first appears."

Mie shrugged. "I don't know when he made arrangements with this person. I don't even remember when they are first in the books. I was introduced to many of his associates, many whom he had dealings with, but he never told me specifically who Baigujing is."

"Because he didn't know," Falco said.

Mie looked at him with a puzzled expression. "I don't understand."

"You are Baigujing."

Mie tried to laugh. "That's ridiculous."

He tossed the open ledger on the table. "You created this person, set up a bank account and paid yourself. When did Lee Jinguo find out?"

Mie's lips squeezed tight. "Okay. Yes. I set up the bank account and began paying myself a small portion. Why not? I was doing the work of a secretary, wasn't I? I deserved something other than a pat on the head. But Jinguo saw me as property, little more than a servant to do his bidding. I was only an ignorant woman to him even though I demonstrated that I had intelligence, that I had education. He didn't care, he just exploited it."

"You never told me how he died," Falco said.

She glared at him. "What does it matter?"

He stood still, staring at her.

"Fine! He was in the garden. He choked while eating fruit."

"Did he find out that you had been taking money?"

"I earned it!"

"But he didn't think that, did he? In his eyes you were stealing from him. You were a dutiful wife who should do what she is told, obey his every word. But you wanted independence. Were you hiding away money so that you could get away from him?"

Her eyes flashed with anger. "That's what I intended, yes."

"But then you didn't have to because he died." He didn't add that it was very convenient that he died after he had discovered her financial indiscretion. He could have suggested that he was murdered but there was no proof that Lee Jinguo's death was suspicious. If he had been helped on his way, it certainly wouldn't have been by the four men whom he was paying off.

"Are you going to accuse me of murder next?" Mie demanded.

Falco shrugged. "No. Lee Jinguo has been dead for two years. Nothing has ever come of it. It may be he deserved what he received, a kind of karma. He was a cruel man. Heartless. An old man who took a teenage wife. He was not a good person, was he?"

"Why did you suspect I was Baigujing? Or that one of the others didn't imprison me."

"Footprints in the dust," Falco said. "The dust in the house was stirred up, but the only distinct footprints were small. They belonged to women, not men. You and Hua-ling."

Anger had started to rise in him, the results of being manipulated, but it evaporated and left only sadness. "You used me, Mie. All this time. You used Hua-ling. I made a promise to you and I fulfilled it. Now it is up to you. I suggest you get out of Nanking. Sell all these businesses. Never get involved with the smuggling or the opium trade again. Go to Europe or America, where no one knows you, where you can start over."

She started toward him but he backed away. Her eyes pleaded with him. "Would you stay with me, John?"

"No." His eyes were cold. The ache in his heart turned it to stone.

Mzoma said, "I do not understand. Who kidnapped Madam Lee?"

"No one," Falco explained, turning from Mie Lee. "She wanted to force me to confront the four men who have been trying to control her. Control her like her husband had."

Mzoma motioned to the young woman on the sofa who was curled in on herself. "But someone hurt Hua-ling."

Falco looked down at the girl with pity. "She did that herself. Right, Hua-ling?"

The girl didn't answer but continued to stare at the floor.

Falco motioned Mzoma toward the door. Together they walked through the ancient house.

"I suspected it when I first heard her speaking Chinese. She's actually Japanese. What she did was something the Yakuza do to offer their leaders undying loyalty. Usually it's because of some indiscretion they have committed. But I suspect in Hua-ling's case it was to demonstrate her loyalty to Mie. They wanted to force me to confront the four. Mie wasn't certain I would be able to do it on my own."

Mzoma took one glance over his shoulder before they left the house. "She doesn't know you very well."

They took a boat back to Shanghai.

Mzoma went to the airfield to arrange flights to Melbourne while Falco returned to the Fairmont Hotel to book adjoining rooms for them. He was still weak and his confrontation with the associates of Lee Jinguo had taken a lot out of him. He hoped to relax for a few hours and return to his exercise routine. A hot bath then some meditation would help. Being back at the Fairmont brought a flood of memories of their last stay, of Kate Murdoch's poisoning him, of his relationship with Mie. He thought he had gained Mie's trust, that they shared a closeness. He had been blind. He had been manipulated. The words of Du Yuesheng came back to haunt him. The gangster had warned him about Mie Lee. Falco should have heeded those words.

When he entered the Fairmont to register, a radiogram was waiting for him at the hotel's front desk.

It was from Flanagan. As the clerk slid his room key across the counter, Falco ripped open the envelope and read the message. He absently took his key as he read the note twice.

Flanagan might not be on the trail of Kate Murdoch after all.

If she was not heading to Australia on that ship, where was she?

But Flanagan finished with an emphatic statement that this was the woman they were searching for. It was merely that the stolen temple items were not on board. He could not locate anything that could be attributed to Kate, nothing that led to her. They had to be on another ship, probably a freighter.

Falco had been convinced that she would not be far from the gold, but he must have been mistaken. Obviously he was terrible at understanding the mind of a woman.

The best he could devise was for Flanagan to keep an eye on her until they were able to get there. If the ship landed before then, Flanagan would have to follow her. She would lead them to the gold artifacts. If she suspected Flanagan, she would disappear again and they would never find the stolen items, including the Buddha for Monk Shi.

Once in his room, Falco's bath was rushed and his meditations were filled with misgivings and disturbing thoughts of failure. He condemned himself for not following after Kate Murdoch himself, though he had been in the hospital at the time and unable to do anything. He had relied on Flanagan and trusted him. He had left it to the Irishman. He should not have gone to Nanking but he had felt obligated to fulfill his promise to Mie Lee. That was done. Now he could concentrate on finding Kate Murdoch if it wasn't already too late.

He pushed himself in his exercises. He was covered in sweat, breathing heavy, when a knock sounded at the door.

William Ewart Fairbairn came in, looking Falco up and down. "You don't look well, John. I heard you were back in town. I thought I'd pop over, see how you were since your brush with death, and fill you in on the update I have about your lady friend."

Falco invited the inspector to a chair, then wiped the sweat from his face with a towel and pulled on a white cotton robe. He ached, but not as much as he had, and the pain in his chest was less noticeable. There was even some times during his exercises that he did not think of Mie Lee. He dropped into the chair opposite Fairbairn.

"What have you got, William?"

"You said this woman went as Sister Catherine, then Kate Murdoch. From her description, I might have narrowed down who she really is. She's spent the last few years in prison in Australia for theft. Her name is Elizabeth Catherine Muldoon originally from Chicago, Illinois. Daughter of Irish immigrants. Bad time for the Irish with the prejudice against them. The father worked all kinds of jobs until he was killed by anti-Irish demonstrations. The mother did everything she could to support her and their daughter, if you take my meaning. Took to liquor and the daughter ran away. Arrested for stealing when she was a teenager. Fourteen. Then she showed up in California two years later. She was in the company of a con artist who was arrested. She was posing as his daughter. Ran away from the foster home. Two years later she was arrested running her own confidence game in Los Angeles. Spent some time in jail there. You get the picture. The arrests are too many for me to remember. Always using an assumed name. When things in the States became too hot for her, she went to Hawaii. Then Australia. She eventually stayed at the behest of the Australian government in one of their facilities. Two years, released a few months ago. Nothing about her since, but I suspect she took on the personae of Sister Catherine to run some new confidence game, part of which was stealing an occasional temple trinket and selling it. When your friend Petrov moved into her territory, she decided to take over his haul. A third of which we were able to send back to Singapore. Is your terrorist friend on her trail?"

Falco pursed his lips. "He believes it's her, under the name of Sister Mary. But he hasn't been able to determine if she has the stolen gold on board or not."

"Where are they headed?" Fairbairn asked.

"Melbourne."

"She knows people there, but they also know her. The police will be able to recognize her even if she is dressed like a nun. Trouble is, she made a lot of friends in prison. If she's got the gold, she'll be able to melt it down soon enough. Then she'll disappear again, maybe South Africa or Europe."

"I can't let her destroy those artifacts, especially the Buddha of Monk Shi," Falco said. "Mzoma has gone to the airfield to see if we can charter a plane."

"Good luck with that, John."

Over the days of a long sea voyage, Flanagan stayed close to Sister Mary. He listened to her talk endlessly about her childhood in California. She was animated, friendly, and talkative. She told him about her service to the Church, helping the poor and needy, of traveling to China to help in an orphanage, then in some hospitals. She had become adept in medical training. She had trained as a nurse before taking vows. She was so convincing Flanagan wondered constantly if she was the person whose history Falco had messaged him in brief before he had begun his arduous air travels, jumping from one airplane to another in a zigzag all over the South Seas. But the most prominent fact about Elizabeth Catherine Muldoon was that she was an accomplished liar. She was an actress of the highest quality who could have performed on stage had she not taken a different path. So he listened to the lies she weaved, trying to find the flaw that would pull the tapestry apart. She was so good he could never catch her and so his doubts would still rage.

Flanagan played his part as the good priest, trying to recall all the things he had learned when he was a boy in church. He held his own. It amused him, two liars playing the parts of pious people of the cloth.

When they landed at Melbourne, he watched Sister Mary leave with her trunk. He was ready, calling for a taxi as soon as hers pulled away.

Flanagan leaped into the back of the cab with his small case.

"Where to, Father?" the drive asked in his local accent.

"Did you see that cab that just pulled away? Could you follow it?"

"The one with the nun in it? Sure, Father. Hang on."

The taxi drove through the early morning traffic of Melbourne, which was sparse and only one other cab was in front of them. The driver had an easy time keeping pace while Flanagan dug into his suitcase. He pulled out a wrinkled brown suit and set it on the seat next to him. His fedora was in even worse shape, but a few punches and manipulations brought it back to life. He pulled off his clerical collar, then began to strip from his black suit.

The driver's eyes kept wandering to his rear view mirror and a puzzled expression became more concerned as Flanagan began to change.

"Keep your eyes on that taxi," Flanagan insisted. "This is a matter of life and death and an extra fiver for you."

The driver nodded and concentrated on the cab he was following.

"Is that nun in danger, Father?"

"More than you can imagine. We might be going into a neighborhood where my collar would stand out and if I'm to help the good Sister, I might need to be invisible. Do you understand?"

"Not really," answered the driver.

"Good. The less you know the better. How would you like to earn some more?"

"Depends."

Flanagan fished into his suitcase and pulled out a scrap of paper and a worn down stub of a pencil. "Just need you to deliver a message for me to the Hotel Windsor. To a man named John Falco."

"Sure."

Flanagan wasn't going to leave Sister Mary to contact Falco. Once Sister Mary reached her destination, Flanagan was not going anywhere. He would keep an eye on her, be her shadow, no matter what. He needed to get a message to Falco once he knew where Sister Mary went. Flanagan had no idea if Falco had made it to Australia as planned, but he was to be at that hotel. Obviously he couldn't meet the ship when it docked or the woman would have recognize him before she revealed where she had the gold. Flanagan had to hope everything had fallen into place.

He watched as the taxi in front of them pulled down a side street and to the front of an old automobile service station. The nun climbed out and spoke to a man in coveralls who was working on a Packard. He wiped his hands on an oil-stained rag.

"Pull to the curb," Flanagan told his driver.

The man nodded and pulled over a block from the garage. Together they watched as the mechanic grinned and greeted the nun. There was a short conversation, after which the man got the steamer trunk from the taxi. The nun paid the driver and the cab drove away.

Flanagan took note of the address of the garage and wrote it down on his note to Falco. He handed it and some bills to the driver.

"Could you also give him my suitcase? If you stick around and drive him back here, I'm sure he'll be most generous in his tip."

The driver took the paper and the money. "Sure, mate. I can do that. Anything to help. You sure she's in danger?"

"That she is," Flanagan said as he opened the rear door, fitting the bent fedora on his red head.

"Good luck to you, Father. Do you want me to notify the coppers?"

Flanagan shook his head. "John Falco works for the police. He'll take care of everything."

As the cab drove away, Flanagan tipped the brim on his hat down to shade his face. He looked around the seedy neighborhood for doorways or alleys he might use to watch the garage. There was a grimy diner he might utilize. He took a cigarette out, put it between his lips, then struck a match. As he touched the flame to the end of the cigarette, he watched Elizabeth Catherine Muldoon follow the mechanic carrying her trunk into the building.

For two hours he strolled from the opening of an alley, to the doorway of an abandoned store front, to the front of a rooming house, continuing to watch the front of the garage. He slipped into the diner for a cup of bitter coffee and watched from a seat at the dirty front window.

When a panel truck pulled up, he wondered if the stolen gold had arrived, or maybe it was merely someone in need of a repair. Then he saw the driver. He was a big black man in coveralls, his muscular arms bare.

Flanagan grinned, dropped a tip on his table next to his cold coffee, and left the diner to walk across the street.

24

When the truck pulled up in front of Jim's garage, Elizabeth Catherine Muldoon heard it rumble to a stop and hurried from the second floor apartment above the garage to the street below. She had changed out of the nun's habit and was grateful for the freedom afforded by the slacks and sweater she now wore. There was some faded paint on the side of the truck, but it had been scraped to the point of unrecognizable gibberish by this time. From it's description it was the truck owned by a friend of Jim, the proprietor of the garage and the brother to Sally, who had been her roommate while a guest of the Australian government's penal system. Sally was finishing her sentence, which allowed Elizabeth to use her bedroom in the second floor apartment until this project was completed. Brother Jim knew people. Unfortunately, not a good lawyer, but he was acquainted with less reputable people who could melt down the stolen gold cups, statues and articles, especially the life-size Buddha that seemed to weigh a ton. She knew it was only coated in gold, but that was still a lot of gold.

Jim had sent his mate with the truck to the docks to pick up the crates. She wanted to be there, wanted to oversee the transfer, to make certain everything went smoothly, but she couldn't. She would be noticed, especially by that red-haired priest. If she was hanging around to watch two big crates of books unloaded from the ship, he might get suspicious and start asking embarrassing questions. She had tried to get rid of him but he had stuck around her all through the voyage even with her talking non-stop. She was starting to run out of things to make up about her life. Her imagination could only create so much.

But he was gone and the crates were here. Soon she would have a fortune in gold and be on her way to Europe. No one knew her in England or France. With this gold to fund her, she could reach the big time in the confidence game. She imagined all the suckers she could run across in Monte Carlo. Big fat bank rolls.

Jim came around from the car he was working on, talking with the big man who had been the driver of the truck. His bare arms looked strong enough to unload the crates himself, but she knew that Jim might have to call for some additional help to get them into the garage until they could arrange for the melting down. She could trust Jim. He was getting his cut. And if he tried to betray her, she had let him know what would happen to his sister. Just to keep Jim honest.

The driver unlatched the truck's back doors and swung them open.

The truck was empty.

No, not empty. In the shadows was a man in a brown suit and a brown fedora, sitting cross-legged on the floor.

As she drew closer to the truck, a familiar voice came from behind her. An Irish lilt.

"I believe you know my friend."

She turned and saw that nosy priest, Father O'Leary. But he was now dressed in a wrinkled brown suit and a battered hat.

"What are you doing here?" she demanded.

Jim started to slide away, sensing a double-cross. The big driver put a huge hand around Jim's upper arm and stopped him from running away.

Elizabeth glared at the priest, who smiled at her.

"Oh, but I'm not really a priest. Same as you weren't really a nun, Elizabeth Catherine Muldoon. I used to know some Muldoons in the old country. Good members of the IRA. Don't suppose you're related. By the way, the names Flanagan. Travis Flanagan. And I believe you've already met my friend Mzoma here. Of course, you're acquainted with my pall Johnny boy, aren't ya?"

Her head spun to the deep shadows of the truck.

The man inside rose smoothly to his feet. She heard his voice echoing through the empty truck. "Hello, Kate."

Impossible! "But … but you're dead."

"You should know," Falco said. "You killed me."

She backed away, bumping into the false priest.

Then there were more people around her. Men in uniform. Men in suits. Everyone was speaking at once. Except for John Falco. He climbed down from the truck to join his two friend while the policemen put handcuffs of her and Jim. He wore a small, insufferable smile and never said a word.

But he was dead. She had seen the newspaper articles. The priest had it when she had first met him after they sailed from Hong Kong. Hong Kong, where Falco lived. The priest, who was really his friend, the Irishman.

She sighed and glared at Falco. She was headed back to prison, back to her cell with Sally.

"How…" she asked Falco on the voyage back to Singapore …"did you survive the poison?"

Falco had booked passage on a steamship to return Elizabeth Catherine Muldoon back to Singapore to answer for murder as well as theft. There were four cabins, two of them connecting. Falco had one connecting cabin, the woman the other. Mzoma and Flanagan had two cabins opposite. Falco was content to allow his two friends to attend to her. Her cabin door was securely locked and bolted on the outside. The port holes were two small even for her to squeeze through. And she was shackled at the ankles.

When she asked the question, Falco was sitting on the deck with crossed legs, trying to meditate. She yelled loud enough from her room that even others along the passageway could have heard.

He didn't answer her. He didn't want to get into a conversation with her.

After a time, she called over. "How did you figure out where the gold was hidden?"

To this question he did reply. It was his attempt to make her feel that she was not as smart as she thought she was.

"Once we knew your real name, it was easy. You had the crates labeled under your father's name. They were supposed to be books.

Only a single layer of old books on top of the artifacts."

"What was the big deal with the gold?" she asked. "Those temples have plenty."

"They didn't belong to you," Falco responded.

"Don't give me that. You were willing to let Mie Lee keep the gold in exchange for the big statue," she disputed. "What is so important about that statue anyway?"

"It is Monk Shi. He belongs at the temple," Falco clarified.

"You mean it's not a statue of Buddha but of some monk? I don't get it."

Falco shook his head, which, of course, she couldn't see. "*No*, you don't," Falco elaborated. "It *is* a statue of Buddha. *Monk Shi* is inside … Believing he had reached enlightenment in his old ages, the monk had himself coated with molten gold to prove himself worthy. The statue is molded around him."

"Inside? A dead monk? That is so grotesque," the woman whined.

"That is why you do not understand," he said.

The next day, he had Mzoma switch cabins.

The day after that, Mzoma insisted that Flanagan retake the adjoining cabin.

When the steamship docked in Singapore, Harold Fairburn, the Inspector-General of Police, met it with a contingent of police officers. After all the other passengers had disembarked, Falco, Mzoma, and Flanagan escorted Miss Muldoon down the gangplank into the waiting arms of the Singapore police.

Fairburn himself faced her and stated, "Elizabeth Catherine Muldoon, in the name of the Straits Settlement, I arrest you for charges of murder, conspiracy to commit murder, and theft. You are to be taken into custody and await trial."

She was marched off under guard while the two crates of cargo were brought out of the ship's hold and loaded onto a truck commissioned by the police.

Falco approached Fairburn. "Inspector, will the gold be impounded as evidence against her?"

"Of course."

"If I may," Falco said, "I would like to request that an exception be made for the Buddha statue of Monk Shi."

Fairburn nodded and gave a small smile. "It's in one of the crates, right? Let me speak to my officers. They will escort you and your friends in one of our cars and the truck will stop at the temple before the crates are impounded … and, Falco," he added, "I had the utmost confidence in you. Thank you."

He reached out his hand, which Falco gripped.

Mzoma sat in the front passenger seat of the police car, with Flanagan and Falco in the back seat. They followed the truck through the streets of Singapore and eventually reached the Twin Grove of the Lotus Mountain Temple.

When the vehicles pulled to a stop, Falco left the vehicle, leaving Flanagan and Mzoma to oversee the removal of the one item.

Falco walked through the temple grounds toward the residence of the abbot but saw Wai Yim walking the garden path and approached him.

He bowed. "Venerable Father, do you remember me?"

The monk smiled. "Of course, my son. Do you bring us any word of our Brother Shi?"

"Please, follow me, my Father," Falco requested.

By the time Falco led the abbot to the front of the temple grounds, the police officers and Mzoma had wrestled the crate from the truck and lifted the statue from the straw bedding to sit it on the grass. At the sight of it, other monks began to gather around.

Wai Yim grabbed hold of Falco's arm and exclaimed: "He has returned!"

The gold statue looked frail and worn, but still shone in brightness with a serene face on it's bowed head and closed eyes, seated in the lotus position. Next to Mzoma Monk Shi was tiny.

When Falco saw it, he placed both palms together and bowed out of reverence. The abbot was also taking the same position, whispering prayers under his breath. Around them, more monks were gathering, each one putting their hands together in prayer of reverence and thanksgiving.

Wai Yim turned to Falco and clapsed his right hand between both of his own. Tears were streaming down his cheeks.

"Thank you, my son. Our Brother Shi is home … Thank you."

Falco felt lighter when he left. The driver of the police car took the three to their hotel while the truck went to the police station with the rest of the stolen gold, to join the portion that had been taken from the junk captain in Shanghai. The lot would all be used as evidence against Miss Muldoon.

Passage on a ship to Hong Kong was arranged for the next day. Falco couldn't return to the island fast enough. His part in this affair was finally over.

He found a copy of *Charlie Chan Carries On* by Earl Derr Biggers in the ship's small library and took to reading it while stretched on a deck chair. He pushed away from his mind the recent events, tried to clear his mind of the woman who tried to kill him, and also the woman who had manipulated him. Mie's image would often appear in his thought, but did not linger. He did not feel anger, for either woman, only a sadness.

Mzoma would often join him while reading a copy of *Ivanhoe* by Sir Walter Scott. He claimed to have read it in his youth at school but remembered little of it. Falco suspected it was to keep him company, to watch over him.

Upon the third day of the voyage, Flanagan, who liked to hang out at the bar and sample their whiskey, joined them on deck with a slip of paper in his hand.

"A radiogram from the great Inspector-General himself," he announced, holding the paper out to Falco who closed his book and stood up. Placing the book on the deck chair, he took the radiogram. Mzoma stood also and the three formed a triangle as Falco read the message out loud.

"Regret to inform you that Muldoon has escaped custody. All of Straits Settlement being searched. No results. Keep you informed."

The End

ABOUT THE AUTHOR

A former pharmaceutical research scientist and teacher, Wayne Carey is the author of the Johnny Falco adventures from Bold Venture Press. These mysteries, set in China of the 1930's, bring back the thrill of the old pulp magazines.

He has continued H. Rider Haggard's famous character with *Allan Quatermain and the Beast Men* and *Allan Quatermain and the Lightning Bird* (Airship 27 Productions). He has written thrillers (*Falco and Company* and *Executive Gambit*, Airship 27), a supernatural (*Company of Shadows*, Airship 27), and several science fiction novels (*Erin, Speaker of the Mihn'd*, Bold Venture Press and *Zombie Island*, Pro Se Productions).

Wayne has contributed to several anthologies, including the award-winning *Legends of New Pulp Fiction* (Airship 27) and *Tales from Plexis* edited by Julie Czerneda (DAW).

Johnny Falco's adventures include *Death Waits in Shanghai*, *Death Comes to Hong Kong*, and the newest series entry *The Gold Buddha.*

ALSO BY WAYNE CAREY:

ERIN: SPEAKER OF THE MIHN'D

A colony world is holding a ceremony honoring an Earth ambassador — who happened to be Erin O'Connor's deadbeat father. Now he's just plain dead. Realizing the event is diplomatic window-dressing, Erin accepts their invitation, hoping the publicity provides a jumping-off point to her own media empire. Hours later, she's a fugitive accused of terrorism — caught between the native Yrrlaar's conflict with the Draq, a reptilian race — and the only person keeping Earth from impending doom?

www.ingramcontent.com/pod-product-compliance
Lightning Source LLC
LaVergne TN
LVHW030911080826
845145LV00010B/2855

* 9 7 8 1 9 6 6 0 8 5 4 7 8 *